Dodge City

ALSO BY PATRICK DEWITT

The Librarianist

French Exit

Undermajordomo Minor

The Sisters Brothers

Ablutions

Dodge City

PATRICK deWITT

4th ESTATE • *London*

4th Estate
An imprint of HarperCollins*Publishers*
1 London Bridge Street
London SE1 9GF

www.4thestate.co.uk

HarperCollins*Publishers*
Macken House
39/40 Mayor Street Upper
Dublin 1
D01 C9W8
Ireland

First published in Great Britain in 2026 by 4th Estate

First published in the United States by Ecco in 2026

1

A catalogue record for this book is available from the British Library

ISBN 978-0-00-878134-7 (hardback)
ISBN 978-0-00-878135-4 (trade paperback)
ISBN 978-0-00-884914-6 (AU and NZ trade paperback)

Designed by Alison Bloomer

Set in Adobe Garamond Pro by Six Red Marbles UK, Thetford, Norfolk

Printed and bound in the UK [using 100% renewable electricity at CPI Group (UK) Ltd]

FSC www.fsc.org
MIX
Paper | Supporting responsible forestry
FSC® C013604

CONTENTS

THE DRAFT NOTICE

LEE CLARKE WOULD LATER THINK OF THE MORNING HE received his draft notice as perceptibly freighted, as though he'd woken up knowing it was on its way to meet his hand; but really it was just another neutral, blinding day in Southern California, his second-floor apartment resting on stilts and leaning toward the greenish, brownish ocean. He was lying in bed, looking up at the ceiling, the minor scents of slow-baking dumpster trash and the rot of low-tide leaking in through the louvered windows. His thoughts were various, ungovernable: he was not in love with Cal, but he did want to take her to the botanical gardens that afternoon. Cal had said she would come to him the night before, and he'd gone to sleep understanding she'd soon arrive and wake him up, but now the night had passed and he was still alone.

The mailman's key-jangling approach brought Lee to a sitting position. He enjoyed watching the delivery of the mail because the previous tenant had drawn a retching face on the door's interior, the mail slot a downturned mouth, so that when the mail came through it looked like the face was spewing onto the parquet flooring. There was the scrape and clack of the slot and now the mail slipped into the apartment. Lee crossed the room, collected the mail, and brought it back to bed with him. At the bottom of the stack was a letter sent by the Selective Service. Lee opened this and learned he'd been drafted to fight in the war in Vietnam, and that he was to report for his physical examination in two weeks' time.

He'd been kicked out of UCLA after an event of violence between himself and another student, and his draft officer had warned him that his deferment status would be lifted. But the officer had given him twelve weeks before he might conceivably receive such a letter, and it had only been six weeks, so it was an unpleasant surprise to find himself in this position. He'd planned on re-enrolling at LACC, but the machine moved with superior speed than he had, and now here was the draft notice, which began with the word, *Greeting*. The absence of an *s* set the letter's tone, which was intended to resound in the mind's ear as the voice of a truth one could not ever get away from: artless, spare, with no trace of comradeship. He read it through several times, then moved to the window, to look out at the ocean, as people like to do in times of strife. He had the sense he'd lost a coin toss but that the terms of the game were far too grave for the method of play—the bingo reality of one draft number meaning life, another death or potential death.

Lee reached for the phone on the floor beside the bed. He called his draft officer Mr. Dewey, but Mr. Dewey didn't pick up and Lee was routed back to a secretary. "How can I help you?" she wanted to know.

"I'm trying to get in touch with my draft officer, Mr. Dewey."

"And what is this concerning?"

"The draft, being drafted."

"Ah," said the secretary. She took down his particulars and said Mr. Dewey would be in touch. Lee hung up and called Cal, but her line was busy. He showered and tried Cal again, but her line still was busy. He was watching the telephone when it rang: Mr. Dewey. Lee had spoken to Mr. Dewey twice before and was struck again by the man's sorrowful gentleness, the seeming misalignment of his temperament and position. Lee explained about the draft notice and Mr. Dewey said, "Now, that's strange."

"Yes," said Lee, nodding. "Because you told me I wouldn't see anything for three months at least."

"That's right, and you shouldn't have."

"So what happened?"

"I can't claim to know, Mr. Clarke."

"But are you saying a mistake's been made?"

"I don't believe I'm saying that, no."

"But you're thinking something can be done?"

"I don't believe I'm saying that, either. Understand that we're talking about a large piece of machinery, here."

"But if something is wrong, it's wrong, right?"

"True enough, as statements go. But I'm not saying this is wrong, I'm saying it's strange."

"But when something is strange, it's because it's wrong."

"I'm disinclined to agree with that. And again, Mr. Clarke, we're talking about a large piece of machinery."

"And what does that mean?"

"It means that a discussion regarding the subtle yet in this case significant difference between strange and wrong is hard to parse in the din."

Lee felt he was being prodded by a stick down a chute and into a black room he was instinctively afraid of, and he made sounds with his mouth and throat that described this feeling. Mr. Dewey had heard these noises before and was not alarmed by them; he spoke calmly as he offered his response: "Here, now. Hold it a minute. Why don't you give me a couple of hours to look into this and I'll let you know what I find out, how does that sound, all right?" He asked Lee to come by his office that afternoon, and Lee said he would be there. He was hanging up when Cal opened the door, watching him with a blank expression as she crossed the entryway and made for the bathroom. She took a forty-five-second shower and came out in a towel. She dropped the towel and got into bed with Lee. "I'm too tired to make love, so you can just forget about that, Lee Clarke." She put his hand on her right breast and it sat there, leaden. She rolled onto her stomach, burying her face in the pillow, voice muffled as she asked, "Who was on the phone?"

"Draft officer."

Cal lay still a moment. "Why were you talking to your draft officer?"

"Because I got my draft notice in the mail this morning."

Cal rose up to rest on her elbow. She asked to see the letter and Lee passed it to her. After she read it she said, "You told me you had time to re-enroll."

"That's what my draft officer had said."

"Did you remind him?"

"Yeah."

"What'd he say?"

"He says it's strange."

"But obviously there's been a mistake. What else did he say?"

"He's looking into it."

She pointed at the letter. "See, he wouldn't be looking into anything if he didn't know they'd made a mistake."

"He's drawing the line at strange." Lee gripped her pointing finger. "I tried to get him to say it was fixable but he wouldn't commit."

"Of course it's fixable."

"Why wouldn't he say so, then?"

"It's fixable, it's fixable." She rolled over and stared at the ceiling, the letter folded in her hand.

"Big night?" Lee asked.

"Regular-sized." After a while she took up the draft notice and reread it. She breathed and thought. "Jesus Christ, Lee!" she said.

CAL

LEE MET CAL AT A HAMBURGER STAND ONE AFTERnoon two years earlier, three weeks after he'd arrived in California from Concrete, Washington. He was slightly drunk and she was very stoned. She was barefoot, and he feigned outrage that society had devolved to the point where a young woman should have her shoes stolen in broad daylight. He bought her a cheeseburger and she ate it. He suggested he might walk her home and she shrugged. The sidewalk was hot; she hopped from one foot to the other and Lee offered to carry her. She stepped up on a bus bench and waved him in, turning him around by his shoulders and climbing onto his back. They set out for her apartment, Cal speaking quietly into his ear: "Left at the stop sign. Right at the liquor store. See that pink building at the end of the block?" She was heavier than she looked, but Lee was rich in the energy his youth afforded him and he kept his struggle hidden away, climbing the steps to her third-floor apartment with a dry brow and only lightly panting. Sufficiently impressed, and recognizing a sport when she saw one, she invited him in, brewed a pot of tea, and made love to him on an uneven pile of pillows on the floor in the living room. Lee was both elated and scandalized; only days prior he had been living in the social reality of small-town America—going steady, with second base the strict border for nice girls, and no clear path to home save a hat-in-hand marriage proposal. Now he looked at his watch and wondered at the fact that ninety minutes earlier he had not known this person existed. They dressed and drank the tea, now gone cold. Cal's attentions drifted and she explained she had homework to do; she was working on a fine arts degree, also at UCLA. Lee walked the ten blocks to his apartment, asking himself how she would describe what had just happened to a third party. That night he felt an agitation of desire that was partly sexual but mostly made up of a curiosity prompted by the look of already-knowing in her eyes. *Cal, huh,* he thought. He returned to her apartment in the morning and she welcomed him in and was friendly to him, but they didn't make love on the pillows, and she addressed him throughout the visit not as Lee but as House Calls. He took this to mean she didn't want him to come unless he was invited, and all through the following long week he was not invited, so he didn't come. Finally there was a knock on Lee's door, and Cal stood with her arms crossed, asking, "Are you House Calls or aren't you?"

She was the daughter of East Coast intellectuals, exotic to Lee in terms of her arcane intellect, just as he was exotic to her in his unspoiled antiurbanity. One morning she informed him he was a patrician redneck; when he asked what that meant she said, "You iron your T-shirts." When he asked if that was good or bad she shrugged and answered, "Who's to say, honey? It's working for me, is all I know." She liked that he was free from ironic detachment, but she also knew he had the raw materials to be whatever stripe of man he wanted to be. She brought him dense books written by touchy men with dire opinions of humanity; she took him to movies that didn't make sense, apparently on purpose. This sometimes led to sidewalk quarrels, with Cal defending this or that filmmaker's aesthetic, and Lee speaking on behalf of clarity and what he called the obligation to the paying customer. He was game to take in all manner of culture, but he had an unshakable sense for order, and more often than not he saw in the obscure a hidden lack in the artist, charlatanry disguised as oracular wisdom. Cal agreed this was a possibility but asked Lee not to use the phrase *paying customer* again, and he promised that he wouldn't.

Cal's friends were a sleazy group, druggy and dark in the eyes, clad in scarves and leather, generally nihilistic in their worldview, and terminally unimpressed with the ample sunshine their location afforded them. They were great ones for asides, sharing their private knowledges with one another but making no effort to conceal Lee's exclusion. None of them appeared to go to school, or hold paying positions; when Lee asked after their life's plans, they couldn't hide their shock of contempt at the banality of the question. What did they say to Cal about Lee when he wasn't around? And what did she say in reply? At the start of their courtship Cal was keen to attempt a blending of Lee's world and theirs; but soon enough she saw the chasm was too vast, and she ceased inviting him around to her apartment, preferring to stay over at his, where such elements couldn't touch them. Sometimes Cal and this grim clique went into the city and she wouldn't come back until the next day, with vague explanations of where she'd been and what she'd done. On such nights, Lee suffered. Cal encouraged him to see other girls if he wanted to, and from time to time he made semiserious attempts at this, but his heart was mired in the older model, the notion of faithfulness and partnership. Cal was sympathetic to a point but she refused to accept anything like criticism from Lee in regards her time away from him.

He held no check over her, and she had told him several times, in the face of his hangdog petulance, that she would understand if he felt he couldn't go through with it. This led to schisms during which time they would not be in touch but invariably, after a few days or a week, they returned to one another with a sense of relief that was mutual and real-feeling, so that neither could deny they were paired, which isn't to say that their relationship was ever going to be free from complication.

One night Lee's phone rang at three o'clock in the morning. It was Cal, and she said, "I'm stranded."

"Stranded where?"

"The Pantry. Can you come get me?"

Lee yawned. "Why don't you ask one of your fuckhead bullshit friends?"

"I don't want to ask my fuckhead bullshit friends, I want to ask you."

"Take a taxi."

"No, you." Her voice was small; something was wrong.

"What happened?" Lee asked.

She sighed. "What happened is past. The pressing contemporary issue is: Are you going to come get me or aren't you?"

"I don't know if I am."

"Right. Well, I'm going to go sit back down and wait for you to figure it out, okay?"

"Okay."

She hung up, and Lee stared at nothing for thirty seconds, then got up and got dressed. It was quiet on the streets; the air held the cold of the ocean, but as he drove inland he could feel the residual warmth of the day coming up off the pavement. He was wearing a white T-shirt, chinos, and dirty white tennis shoes without socks. The windows were down and everything was making just enough sense for him to feel more or less serene.

Cal was sitting at the lunch counter next to a late middle-aged man with a sunworn face and a frayed straw hat perched at the back of his head. He was describing large and consequential movements with his hands; Cal was smiling sleepily up at him, her chin resting on her palm. When she saw Lee approaching, she straightened, pointed, and said to the man, “I told you! Pay up!” Her eyeliner was smudged, her hair was bent; clasping Lee’s bicep, she said, “This is Duke. He knows all about farm equipment.”

Duke shook Lee’s hand. “Industrial farm equipment.” He pulled out his wallet and passed a dollar bill to Cal, who explained to Lee, “We had a bet about whether or not you’d show.” Now Duke stood away from his stool, grinning at Cal and Lee. “Go get ’em, little babies,” he said. After he left, Cal paid for her coffee with the dollar, then she and Lee walked out to the Ford, not talking. As Lee turned west on Olympic, Cal lay her head on his lap and shut her cycs.

"Hey," said Lee.

"What."

"What happened?"

"Bad time."

"Are you okay?"

"Yeah."

"Is there someone I'm supposed to kill?"

"No, it's not like that."

They drove in silence. She was asleep by the time they got back to the beach, and in the morning she wouldn't be drawn out other than to say she should've known better, and that she wouldn't make the same mistake again.

There were further incidents. They went to an apartment-warming party in Santa Monica for a school friend of Cal's. Lee and Cal were sitting on the couch chatting with the host when Cal suddenly grew rigid. Lee looked up and saw a man standing across the room staring at Cal in a state of anguish. Cal whispered to Lee, "Do me a favor, pretend you're my boyfriend." As Lee sat with his arm draped protectively over Cal's shoulder he cycled through the emotions of confusion, shame, outrage. The anguished man soon left the party and Cal relaxed, kissing Lee on the cheek and thanking him. Lee withdrew into a sulk; driving home, Cal asked Lee what he was unhappy about.

He said, "When do you want me to stop pretending?"

"Pretending what?"

"That I'm your boyfriend."

She turned to look at him. "Whenever you want."

"And what if I don't want to stop?"

"Then don't."

Cal saw Lee as a model of 1950s masculinity, and while she couldn't deny her desire for and enjoyment of him, she was a little disappointed in herself that she had succumbed to the antique figurehead. Lee saw Cal as a winning combination of sex appeal and intelligence. He admired her, and her influence made him glad, uneasy. They eventually came to an agreement of monogamy, at least according to the standards of the era, but there was no discussion between them relating to anything other than the present and immediate future. It was both complex and simple at the same time, and Lee sometimes wondered if he wasn't better off out of it. But he did love Cal, no matter what he told himself when he was alone.

THE EVENT OF VIOLENCE

LEE HAD COME TO STUDY AT UCLA NOT OWING TO ANY scholastic ambition but because the school's location appealed to his sense of adventure. He took as his major land surveying, something he was not particularly interested in, and something he might just as easily have studied at the University of Washington in Seattle. But he was keen to experience new social systems, and to get out from under the permanent gray ceiling of Washington state. He had arrived in Los Angeles in the Ivy League uniform he'd assembled ahead of his departure from Concrete: the sport coat and button-down Arrow shirt, the medium-wide necktie, cuffed slacks, penny loafers. He wished to impart seriousness, maturity; almost as soon as he arrived in Los Angeles, however, he understood that he was fully a step behind. In the summer of 1965, one did not yet see men in flowing robes with hair to their shoulders, but that aesthetic element was forming, a culture coming into bloom. Lee couldn't fully grasp what it was all about; those taking part spoke of a new stripe of freedom, a freedom unknown to their forebears, and this sounded positive to Lee. But it also seemed to be some kind of antihygiene movement, and Lee, having grown up in a working-class household, was prohygiene. Despite this, there was an instinctive appeal to the notion of uncharted behaviors, and across his first year in Los Angeles, and by way of Cal's casual guidance, he'd let his hair grow an inch or two longer than he had before, and he did away with the Vitalis and cologne.

Cal had one foot in her studies and one in the new freedoms camp, and she spoke to Lee of what was coming up for the youth of America and the world. "According to the architects, it's going to be a complete undressing of moral tradition and societal standards, with nothing forbidden save forbidding. The ultimate aim, they say, is universal love."

"Which is what?"

"Everyone takes everyone else at face value and accepts them for who they are, damaged, imperfect, the works."

"Just like that."

"They're not saying it's not going to be a process."

"The architects aren't."

"No."

"But do you believe in it?"

"Let's call it a tall order."

"Impractical."

"Sure."

"Where do you see it going?"

She nodded. "Once the money pigs figure out a way to turn a profit off the culture, and it's going to take about ten seconds, they will, then the whole thing'll eat itself and collapse under the weight of its own disorderly excess."

"Then what?"

"A great overcorrection in the opposite direction and it'll be worse than it ever was."

"Is the new freedom movement itself an overcorrection?"

"Yes."

"You're not making a very strong case for taking part."

"You should take part because it's going to be fun."

"But I'm already having fun."

"New freedoms, new fun," she said. "Better fun, funner fun."

It was Cal who had invited Lee to the party that led to the event of violence. The party took place in a haggard old mansion on the edge of the UCLA campus. Lee arrived alone, entering the house with a six-pack under his arm and stepping into a bank of smoke. Several of these new freedom types were in attendance, but Lee could place none of them as being linked to Cal. He was aware that his presence as an outsider, and one not directly engaging with the culture, was causing little ripples of discomfort among the attendants, and he tried to make his face easy to show them he was peaceable. He looked into this and that room but couldn't find Cal. He came into the mansion's main parlor, where the new freedom crowd had gathered around a sectional, twenty or more of them, eyes blurred, mouths fixed in scowlish smiles.

"Cal?" he called, to no response. "Has anyone seen Cal?"

"Cal Worthington?" asked a sneering voice.

Lee sat in an itchy love seat, its arms wrapped in duct tape, and he popped the top on a can of beer. The group was studying him frankly, now; one among them stood out as the leader, a rangy, handsome blond with shaggy hair and a beard, so much as he could grow one. He was wearing sandals. That a grown man would expose his feet in a public setting went against Lee's sense of propriety, and he felt shame on the man's behalf. The blond was staring at Lee.

"Want a beer?" Lee asked.

"No thanks, Dad," the blond answered. He stood up

from the group and came to sit on the floor before Lee, legs folded, a joint in his hand.

"Why don't you pull up a seat," said Lee.

"I've got a seat."

"You're sitting on the floor."

"I sit on the earth."

"It's linoleum."

The blond smoked his joint and watched Lee drinking his beer. The way he looked at Lee was hard, but the blond, Lee could see, was soft. What he possessed was boldness. His acolytes, likely used to such performances as this, were snickering nervously. Something was happening, and the herd was anxious in its waiting for the something to materialize. Their silence made space for the realization of the interaction.

"Well, how you doing?" Lee asked.

"Just fine," the blond answered. "How are you?"

"Also fine."

"Feeling normal?"

"Sure."

"You're feeling the normality?"

"Sure."

"He's normal, he's feeling it," the blond said over his shoulder. He took a big swallowing hit off the joint and held it out for Lee. Lee had smoked marijuana three or four times but found it made him dislike himself, and so he'd sworn it off. He held up his beer, wagging the can; the blond said, "That stuff's no good."

"It makes me sing and dance," Lee said.

This provoked a laugh among certain of the new freedom types, surprised by Lee's show of spirit. The blond waved his crowd down and turned back to Lee, leaning in. "Can I ask you something?"

"Sure."

"Why are you here?"

"Same reason as you, I'd imagine."

"That's doubtful."

"Is it?"

"Highly doubtful."

"Perhaps you have a doubting nature."

"Why don't you answer the question."

"Okay. I was told there was a party, and here I am."

"But who invited you?"

"Cal."

The blond looked over his shoulder. "Is there a Cal here? There's no Cal here." He turned back to Lee. "Where are you from, even?" he asked.

"I live in Venice."

"No, man. Where are you *from*?"

"All right. You'll enjoy this. I'm from Concrete, Washington."

This brought a long smile to the blond's face. He pointed a finger at the sitting figure of Lee. "This man is a

Concretian," he told his crowd. "He drinks a golden elixir from the aluminum well of his father's father's father."

The laughter among the group was the relieved laughter that accompanied victory, and Lee decided it was time to go. There were too many of them to face down, and he felt there was no way he might redeem himself, retreat the only option other than violence, which seemed inappropriate in the setting. "Right," he said, standing up from the love seat.

"You're not leaving?" the blond asked, mock-crestfallen. "We're just getting to know each other."

"I've got to get going. If you see Cal, tell her I've come and gone."

"Cal Worthington?" the sneering voice repeated. The laughter was ongoing and the blond in particular was joyous in his domination, calling out to Lee's retreating figure, "Stay! Tell us of your traditions and rituals! Take us to your neon cave paintings! Sing us a selection from the songbook of the factory floor!" Lee left the party hot in the face, the cackling ringing in his ears. He crossed the street and sat in his car and drank the rest of his six-pack, picking out clever rejoinders he might have offered up to the blond, but these were a cold comfort, and anyway, there was no way to win an argument of wits with a group so certain of their rightness. Soon the beer was gone, and Cal still nowhere in sight. Lee was warming up the Ford for the drive home when he saw the blond, alone now, leaving the party. Lee watched him, disliking everything about him, even the way he moved, with an affected slouch, as if the very idea of good posture was old guard. The blond walked up the sidewalk and toward campus. Lee turned the car off. He slipped out onto the sidewalk, following quietly, at a distance.

Fistfights among the boys and men of Concrete were common enough, and Lee had fought more times than he could recall, but he was not one who had enjoyed these exercises, was not by nature one who often rose to anger, and he'd not been in a fight or anything like a fight since he left Washington state two years earlier. But he understood he would now endeavor to harm the blond with physical violence, and while he did not excite at this, neither was he afraid. It seemed a necessary errand, a chore that needed doing. The campus was quiet, empty, dark; Lee increased the pace of his step and as he drew near, the blond heard his footfall, paused, and turned. Squinting at the approaching silhouette, he asked, "Concrete? What are you doing?"

There was a style of man who needed to work himself into a lather ahead of a fistfight, usually by way of threatening language and vulgarity; but Lee had always felt such performances marred the clean communication of violence, and he said nothing in answer to the question. The blond was shifting in his sandals. There was, at the edge of his conscious mind, the understanding that he was on the cusp of ceding control; but still and he clung to his wise attitude, his belief he was safe in his superiority. "You're not thinking of dusting off the masculine bloodletting performance, are you? The Cro-Magnon song and dance?" Lee hit him in the teeth with a straight right and the blond dropped to the ground, where he lay stilly, soundless as snowfall. Lee supposed the blond was doing some thinking, and he took a moment to bask in the quiet, the moment so very free from smart aleckry. He turned and walked back the way he'd come, driving home in silence and arriving in a fine mood, easy in his heart and thinking of the blond almost not at all. There was a divot in his right knuckle and he cleaned the wound with hydrogen peroxide and patted it dry with toilet paper. He got into bed and soon fell asleep. Cal let herself in after 2 a.m.; she woke him by shaking his shoulder. "What's all this blood?" She turned on the bedside lamp, tracing the blood to Lee's hand. "Lee?" Lee explained about the event of violence. Cal said she knew who the blond was, and said it was a long time coming; but he was, she said, the vindictive type, which wound up being prophetic.

It was the naming of Concrete as Lee's point of origin that would prove his undoing. He was the only student enrolled in the college to have come from the town; the day after the event of violence he was called away from class and to the dean's office, where the blond sat quietly, in sunglasses, and with a purple blemish of bruising across his swollen lips. Lee greeted the blond in a casual tone and asked if he'd come from a pie-eating contest. "None of that," interrupted the dean, snapping his fingers for silence. Pointing at Lee, he asked the blond, "Is this the boy who struck you?" The blond nodded that it was, and the dean said he could go. After the blond left, the dean explained to Lee that the blond's parents were esteemed benefactors. He didn't seem at all upset about the violence but there was, he said, a bottom line to consider, and that he hoped Lee understood his position.

"What's your position?" Lee asked.

"Of course you're expelled," said the dean.

"Expelled or suspended?"

"Expelled."

"When am I expelled?"

"Right now."

Lee thought about what this meant. That he did not have any true passion as regards his studies was, he told himself, beside the point. He remembered the draft, then; but that was something in the far distance. He asked if there was anything that needed doing in response to the expulsion and the dean said he couldn't think of anything, and he stood and shook Lee's hand and wished him all the luck. "All the luck," he said. Lee walked off campus and drove home and waited around for Cal to come by so that he could fill her in.

DRAFT OFFICER DEWEY

THE MORNING HAD BEEN SPOILED BY THE ARRIVAL OF the draft notice. Lee was too upset to make love, and Cal soon gave up trying and went to sleep while Lee moved to the kitchen, drinking bitter coffee and explaining his options to himself, which were few enough, and each one characterized by its own special unpleasantness. He dressed and drove the Ford to the campus at Los Angeles Community College, enrolling in a full set of general education courses and tucking away the receipt with the draft notice. He visited a barbershop on Vermont and had his hair trimmed; he stopped at Desmond's on Wilshire, purchasing a sport coat on credit, then drove in the direction of the induction center, but roundaboutly, on surface streets, with time to kill, and still turning the matter over in his mind. Idling at a red light he was taken up by a fearful amazement, recognizing that he was pinned to the ground, and with no mercy forthcoming.

The induction center was a few miles inland from Lee's neighborhood; he arrived to find a group of draft resisters assembling in advance of a protest. Lee parked up the block and passed through the loose crowd, making for the center's entrance. He was halfway up the steps when someone caught his arm; he turned to find his friend Robin looking up at him. Taking in Lee's conservative clothing and hairstyle, Robin said, "My good man, what have they done to you?"

One day, a year or so earlier, Lee came upon someone inspecting the Ford's engine. Thinking the figure a battery thief, Lee offered up a vulgar threat as he drew near; Robin came out from under the hood, smiled sincerely. "No need for that. I'm an admirer of yours." He'd been passing by after a session at the beach break out front of Lee's apartment; when he saw the Ford, immaculate in the late morning haze, he couldn't help but investigate. "I knew the engine would be a treat, but I just had to see for myself. No hard feelings, right?" Lee shook Robin's hand, chilled from the ocean. His hair was wet and stringy and he wore canvas board shorts, nothing else, and he looked as naturally elegant as a panther resting in a tree. When

Lee pulled a toolbox from the trunk of the Ford, Robin asked him what he was going to get up to.

"Oil change, plugs and points," said Lee.

"Mind if I hang around?"

"I don't think I mind." This was good enough for Robin, who dashed off to stash his board in his van, returning in the same damp shorts, but with a T-shirt and sneakers rounding out the ensemble. They spent the next eight hours together, wrenching on the car and driving up and down the coast, drinking Stroh's, and speaking of their lives. Until recently, Robin had been enrolled in the dramaturgy program at UC Irvine, but he'd found it a stiflingly conservative environment and so had dropped out, and now he was living in his van, surfing and working on a play taking place across the space of a single night after hours in a city zoo. Robin and Lee's conversations always came around to the state of the play; on the steps of the induction center, Lee asked again after its progress.

"Very much coming together," Robin answered, nodding vigorously. "I've decided it's going to be a musical, with all the animals singing different songs from their individual cages."

"Who's writing the songs?"

"I am."

"I didn't know you were a songwriter."

"Neither did I."

Lee said, "Are the animals puppets, or people in costumes?"

"I think costumes. But I also like the idea of the singers hiding behind the puppets and throwing their voices out into the darkness, so I don't really know." Lee noticed that Robin was holding two bananas in his left hand. Robin noticed his noticing and asked, "Want one?"

"No thank you."

Robin began peeling a banana for himself. He took a bite and said, "There's a regular human character too, the night watchman. He comes and goes."

"Is he friendly or unfriendly?"

"With the animals? Friendly, but not hugely. He's got problems of his own."

"What are his problems?"

"In a nutshell: ennui." Robin took another bite of the banana.

"Do the animals talk to him?"

"Yeah, but he can't understand them."

"Does he talk to the animals?"

"Yeah. They *can* understand him."

"Does the night watchman sing?"

"You bet he does."

"What's the mood of the songs?"

"Various, just like real life." He pointed the banana stump at the induction center, looming behind Lee. "Hey, though."

"What?"

"Did you get one too?"

"One what?"

"You know. It comes in the mail and doesn't go away?"

"I got one, yeah. You?"

"Sir yes sir, I surely did. I'd thought they couldn't get at me because I'm living mobile, but they sent it to my folks'."

"What do you think?"

"I think 'what do you think?' is the primary question at hand. Off the top of my head I'd say I have a hard time imagining my going over there."

"But are you saying you won't go?"

"I'm saying I'd like to try to avoid it."

This led to the naming of all the methods for flunking one's induction. These tales were passed around among the young draftees of America: men arriving for their physicals in women's lingerie; men feigning belief they were pharaohs; men staying up for five straight nights on amphetamines and allowing the temporary psychosis to repel the induction bosses. Robin liked such stories, and in the past Lee hadn't disliked them, but he knew he could never muster one of these life-or-death performances, and he said as much to Robin, who asked, "You think dressing up like a weatherman's going to get you off?" Lee said that that was the plan, and looked at his watch. "I don't want to be late. You going to be here awhile?"

Robin scanned the landscape, pointing at a sickly city tree, stooped and dusty, thirsty in the distance. "There."

Lee climbed the stairs and entered the induction center. It was quiet, cool, and instantly upsetting. He met a small man at a large desk who asked after his purpose. Lee began to explain about the draft notice and the man cut him off with a give-me gesture. Lee produced and passed over the letter and the man looked at it and told Lee he was two weeks early. Lee said he had an appointment with Mr. Dewey and the man asked him why he hadn't said so in the first place and Lee said he didn't know why. He was directed to an office deep within the body of the building where the secretary to Mr. Dewey, a medium-size man at a medium-size desk, also asked to see the draft notice. "You're two weeks early," he said. Lee again explained about the appointment with Mr. Dewey, and the secretary checked the statement against Mr. Dewey's appointment book. "Oh yes, there you are," he said, as if pleasantly surprised. He pointed to a row of chairs set against the wall and asked Lee to sit. Having nothing else to do, Lee made a study of the room, an area whose defining characteristic was its noncharacteristic: the colors of paint were not meant to be smart or attractive, but invisible, to be no color at all. There were no plants in the room, no magazines to flip through; the overhead lighting was severe and produced an even, mildly unplcasant humming buzz. The chairs were sturdy but without adornment, no armrests, and minimally cushioned, making no invitation to loiter. The lone aesthetic gesture rested on the wall high above the secretary: a framed lithograph of a heroic eagle, descending from above in what looked to be a rage of activated patriotism. Its talons were blood-dipped, a fresh kill in the immediate past, with further violence soon to come, judging by its dive-bombing posture. The eagle's face was the portrait of ferocity but there were also, Lee noticed, beaded tears in the corners of its eyes. The eagle, he deduced, was having a two-sided emotional experience, at once homicidal and reverent, moved by his own willingness to defend his homeland, but also by the righteous nationalism his willingness rested upon. A banner unfurled about the eagle's lower body: TO A MAN, FREE. Lee read the banner five and six times, and he understood he had entered a lunatic reality, understood that he was in danger to be standing among such men as these who believed that the eagle image was suitable for framing, or that any room on earth should feel the way this room felt. A brief and startling buzzer sounded, summoning a flinch in Lee. The secretary told him, "You can go in now," and Lee crossed under the gaze of the eagle and into Mr. Dewey's office.

Mr. Dewey was a large man at a small desk drinking coffee from a paper cup and wearing the worn-down eyes of the individual who had come a long way for not so very much. This was the mouthpiece of the American military organization, and he proposed that Lee should make himself comfortable, and Lee sat in the uncomfortable chair and said, "Thank you." Mr. Dewey asked to see Lee's draft notice and Lee passed this over, along with the receipt from LACC, explaining that he'd re-enrolled. Mr. Dewey had nothing to say to this. He glanced briefly at the paperwork and handed it back to Lee. "I looked into your case file, Mr. Clarke, and could find nothing related to the fact of your being taken off the deferment list. By which I mean to say that I have no satisfactory answer to give you at the moment. I named twelve weeks as the period of time you might re-enroll because that was what you were meant to be given. The reason why you were given less, if there is a reason at all, is not written into the text of your file."

He opened up the file on his desk and peered over it. "I see that you were expelled, but the reason for your expulsion is not named here."

"I struck a student on campus, sir."

"Did you?"

"Yes."

"That's interesting." Mr. Dewey took up a pencil and began writing in the file's margins.

Lee asked, "Interesting how, sir?"

"Interesting generally."

"But, do you think there could be a connection?"

"Between what and what?"

"Between the reason for my expulsion and my being taken off the deferment list."

"I see what you mean." Mr. Dewey completed his notation and set his pencil down. "You're imagining a group whose goal is the seeking out of those citizens already familiar with violence, that they might be pivoted or guided in the direction of a combat zone?"

"It sounds paranoid if you say it like that."

"I can tell you that it would be highly challenging to assemble such a group, Mr. Clarke, as it would involve a large body, scattered thinly with many isolated players, which always brings a likelihood for information bleedage. Also, and to the side of our discussion, it takes more than a knowledge of violence to make a soldier. There is wheat and chaff after all, yes?"

"Yes."

"The very idea that we are hoping to align with the violence-inclined is a misrepresentation. The preexisting inclination toward violent behaviors is actually a strike against a young man hoping for a place in the armed forces."

"Okay."

"Not to say we're courting pacifists."

"No," said Lee. "And so you're telling me you have no theories or ideas about why I've been called up prematurely?"

"It's uncommon but not unheard-of. We're talking about the stroke of a pen, here."

"A mistake."

Mr. Dewey paused. "I sympathize with your ongoing desire to hear me say that word, Mr. Clarke, but you will not hear it, not from me you won't. Call it poor luck if you must, or fate's ungenerous hand, but I see no evidence of error."

"What about my re-enrollment?"

"It's too late, I'm afraid."

"What if I get married?"

"Too late."

Lee sat for a time under the dome of his disappointment, and it seemed that Mr. Dewey would allow Lee to sit thus, in silence, for however long he wished. But there came an interruption from beyond the office, from outside the building, the growing sound of the protest, now underway. Mr. Dewey was looking in the direction of the noise, a trace of amusement evident in his expression as he asked Lee, "Are you one of these?"

"No, not really."

"I didn't think so. Naturally, my side wants to write them all off as cowards, though it may be more complicated than that."

"Speaking for myself, I can say that my feelings about being drafted are definitely informed by fear."

"No one is asking you not to be fearful, but that you master your fear."

"But you're bringing us fear we don't ask for or want or have room for."

Mr. Dewey turned away from the sound of the protest, watching Lee with a look of friendly incredulity. "You sound just like a child," he marveled. "Look: Would you agree that there's a social contract between the government and its citizens?"

"I would agree to that."

"Are you all not breaking the social contract by refusing to come to the aid of your country when your country needs it?"

"The service that you're asking feels beyond the boundaries of our relationship."

"There is no boundary. We're all one entity."

"There's a boundary."

"There's not." He pointed in the direction of the protesters. "They tell themselves they're apart, and maybe they are, but it's owing to their own decisions. These people are a haircut and thirty-dollar suit away from a job in government service."

"They don't want a job in government service."

"That's not the point."

"They don't want to go to Vietnam."

"Very few people *want* to go to Vietnam, Mr. Clarke, even those with faith in the cause."

Lee said, "Okay, but what if somebody *really* doesn't want to go?"

"This is not uncommon, and is one of many wrinkles ironed out across the course of basic training."

"But they can't make someone fire a weapon."

"Actually, the newest data points to a three-fourths conversion rate from Reluctant to Effective Combatant. In other words, they can."

Lee said, "Mr. Dewey."

"Mr. Clarke," said Mr. Dewey.

"I do not want to go to Vietnam."

"No. I'm sensing that."

"But what can I do?"

"What indeed."

"Yes, what?"

"Well," said Mr. Dewey, and he held out his hands to show there was nothing in them.

Lee asked, "Am I going to Vietnam, Mr. Dewey?"

"Is there anything physically or mentally wrong with you?"

"No."

"Then I'd say that yes, you are."

"When?"

"Physical in two weeks, induction two weeks later, followed by eight weeks of basic training, then eight weeks of infantry training. After that you've got thirty days at home, then you're on a plane."

"And you believe I'll see combat?"

"That would be your function, yes."

"Okay. Well. Thank you."

"You're welcome."

"Goodbye."

"Good day."

Lee left the room, stepping dazedly down the long hall, through the marble mezzanine and to the exit. He stood at the top of the stairs looking out, over and past the protest. He walked down the steps, pausing at the edge of the crowd. He removed his sport coat, still crisp in its newness, and dropped it into a metal-mesh trash can. The trash can was near to full and Lee stood awhile, watching the balled-up coat resting atop the garbage. Before him stood the mass of protesters, several hundred young men and women waving their banners and invoking their slogans, canny little phrases written in criticism of the very thing that had just happened to Lee, for all the good it did him.

There was no going around the protesters, so he picked his way through them, and he saw the crowd broken down to its individual units, the eyes and faces, the teeth and tongues and gums, the chanting, shouting mouths, their volume and wind. Certain of the chantmakers seemed to be embellishing or performing their outrage, and Lee wondered if they weren't making themselves foolish in the eyes of nature.

Robin was not standing beneath the sickly tree, but Lee found his banana peel. Approaching the Ford, Lee saw Robin sitting in the passenger seat, eating his second banana and waving. When Lee got in the car, Robin told him, "You look like the little old lady who just got flashed."

"It's scary in there."

"Did you get it sorted out?"

"There's no sorting it out, I don't think."

"They've got you?"

"As far as they're concerned."

"They give you an induction date?"

"One month."

"Goddamn."

"Yeah."

"That's soon, Lee."

"I know."

"What are you going to do?"

"I don't know. What are *you* going to do?"

Robin said that he didn't know either, but began casting about for some answer to the question: there were doctors reputedly selling 4-F deferments; there were resistance organizations offering all manner of assistance to conscientious objectors—he was only looking for some glinting light to be heartened by, but his words reeked of doom to Lee. It occurred to Lee that he had known, from the moment he first read his draft notice, that there was only one sensible response to such a thing. Having now arrived at the place of irrevocability by way of his meeting with Mr. Dewey, Lee understood the time to be sensible had come. He was looking up the road at the shifting border of the body of protesters. "You still want to buy my car?" he asked.

"Yes, shit, sure I do. Are you serious?"

"Yeah. But do you have any money?"

"I have some."

"How much?"

"How much for the car?"

"It's worth five hundred."

"I don't have that much."

"How much do you have?"

"Two hundred? Almost two hundred?"

"I need five hundred."

"Can I get it to you later?"

"I need it now."

"When's now?"

"Tomorrow."

Robin took the last bite of his second banana, rolled down the window, dropped the peel in the gutter, rolled the window back up, lit a cigarette and smoked awhile, looking Lee up and down. "You're dodging," he said.

Lee looked back at Robin but said nothing.

Robin asked, "You gonna walk to Canada?"

"I've got seventy dollars to my name."

Robin nodded and said, "I think I can get the money. I'll let you know one way or the other by tomorrow, all right?"

"What time tomorrow?"

"Let's say lunchtime."

"Lunchtime not dinnertime."

"Lunchtime, lunchtime." Robin hopped out of the Ford, disappearing into the crowd. Lee drove home to find the bed empty and neatly made, a note from Cal on the pillow: *Find me, tell me.* Lee called her number but there was no answer. He walked to her apartment and knocked but she wasn't home. He returned to his apartment and spent the next few hours drinking beer and weeding through his possessions, allotting himself one large suitcase. It was pleasing, in some way, to do this; to break down one's worldly goods to the fundamental. He set the suitcase by the front door and went out for Chinese food. When he came back there was a second note on top of the first: *Where are you?* He called Cal but she didn't answer. He went to sleep and Cal came in after 2 a.m., drunk and stoned and telling herself small comical secrets. She opened and closed the refrigerator, took a brief shower, then got into bed, naked and damp, sticking Lee in his side with her thumb.

"Are you awake?"

"No."

"Wake up. What happened?"

He rolled over and looked at her. "I told them how cute you are and they're going to call off the war on our behalf."

"Tell me, Lee."

"Ah," he said.

"What?"

"It's no good."

"What's that mean?"

"They've got me."

She reached up and grabbed a handful of his hair in her tightening fist.

"It's no good and they've got me and I'm leaving, Cal. And that's just the end of it."

There came after this a long phase of not talking in the dark, followed by an equally long phase of talking. The question of whether or not Cal might come along was not asked; it seemed the answer was already written, and so neither of them could give voice to it. They returned to not talking, which was better than the other as there were no words to change what had happened and what would keep happening to them. Eventually Cal decided they should make love but Lee didn't want to, or felt that he couldn't. Cal was persistent, though, and soon Lee did want to and could, but then Cal started crying at the midpoint and so Lee couldn't anymore and they gave it up as a lost cause. There was a phase of holding each other, then not holding each other, and they were apart in the dark. There was nothing to be done; it was over, simply, and it was.

THE RUNNING-AWAY-FROM-AMERICA PARTY

CAL WAS FEELING SICK IN THE MORNING. SHE STAYED in bed while Lee went about performing the business of dismantling his life. Sitting at the kitchen table, he made a list of to-dos. The first on the list was *quit job*; he took to the phone and called Mr. Headley, who asked, "Since when are you a telephone guy?"

"I've got some bad news, Mr. Headley."

"What's the matter? You got the shits?"

"No, it's that I'm quitting."

Mr. Headley paused. "Why would you want to do something like that?" Lee explained about his being drafted, and Mr. Headley said, "But you're giving me two weeks, right?"

"In two weeks they'll be shaving my head."

"Wow. Okay. Some fine way to start the day."

"I'm sorry. I wish I didn't have to do it."

"No, hell, kid. If you're drafted, you're drafted. I mean as excuses go, you're in good stead with me. You want me to mail your check or you coming in for it?"

"I'm coming in. I was hoping for cash, if that's all right."

"Sure it's all right."

"Thanks."

"Of course, kid. It's a fine thing you're doing."

"Okay, Mr. Headley. I'll see you."

Lee hung up and drew a line through *quit job*. Beneath *quit job* was *bus/plane/train?* He hauled out the Yellow Pages to check the prices of these three modes of travel, going one way from Los Angeles to Vancouver. He was studying the notes he'd made of the particulars when Robin came into the kitchen by way of the back door. He poured himself a cup of coffee and sat at the table opposite Lee, his face expressing its typical eerie serenity. After Lee told Robin what he was doing, Robin became activated, and now the pair of them fell into a discussion of the particulars of each mode—considerations of economy, comfort, and aesthetics. The primary detractor, it seemed to Lee, was a feature of each of the modes: there would be no chance for diversion, pause, or whim. The draft notice had stripped him of something he'd never considered a luxury before, which was his agency; now that he was leaving, a desire rose up in him to maintain some level of control in terms of the specifics of his departure. As Lee described the sentiment, a look of concern clouded Robin's face. "This isn't where you tell me you're not selling the car anymore, I hope."

"I have to sell it. Are you still buying it?"

Robin's voice was solemn. "The funds have been secured."

Lee held his hand out, palm up: pay me. Robin held his hand up, palm facing Lee: wait. "I don't have the money on my person at this current particular moment in time. But my old man's good for it, and he understands about the deadline."

"Cash by the end of the day?"

"Tomorrow morning at the latest, after the banks wake up." Robin reached for Lee's notepad, looking over the columns and figures. "Nice penmanship, Lee," he said.

"Thanks."

"I'm serious. Consistent, elegant yet legible—very nice." He took up Lee's pencil and began filling in the zeros with an even shading. "Hey, why don't you sign on for a drive-away?"

"I've never done one of those before."

"It's not complicated. All you've got to do is connect the car to its destination, more or less on time and unsmashed." Robin commenced flipping through the Yellow Pages. "Hand me the phone."

"I don't want to get signed up for anything."

"Let's just see what's available."

Lee passed the phone to Robin. Robin picked up the receiver and dialed a number. "Yes, hello, good morning, how are you?" Using Lee's name, he described himself as a seminary student taking the semester off to see the country. He stated that he had no desired destination, but that he preferred the climate of the northern states, and that he wished to leave as soon as possible. The first agency had nothing to meet the specifications, neither did the second, but with his third call Robin suddenly was taking notes and asking cryptic questions about mileage allowances and delivery timelines. After he hung up he told Lee, "Bonanza."

"Yeah?"

"Yeah. Three options, all right?"

"Right."

"Option one's going to Bellingham, but it's a fifteen-year-old Plymouth station wagon. Not ideal in terms of make, but it'll get you where you want to go and it sounds like there's some leeway regarding the delivery date. Option two's a newer model Mercury, but that's a copilot situation."

"What's that mean?"

"Means the owner's in the car with you. And while it could be a horny swanlike heiress, more than likely it'll be a dead-assed suburban cheapskate with opinions to burn."

"Where's that one going?"

"Bismarck, North Dakota. You got a map?"

Lee fetched an Esso map and laid it out across the kitchen table. Robin located Bismarck and pointed. "Puts you close to the border, only you're landing in the middle of Saskatchewan, no offense to Saskatchewan. But that's a long ways away from either coast, and I imagine you'd rather land in a larger city, or nearer to one, right?"

"I think so, yeah," said Lee. "And what's the third option?"

"The third option's the one I'm most interested in."

"Okay."

"There's a plus and a minus with the third option. But the plus is significant. And the minus has potential to transform to plus, depending on your mental attitude."

"What's the minus?"

"The car's due in New Jersey."

"That's too far," said Lee.

"Too far for what?"

"Too far to drive. Too far from Canada."

"Toronto's a day's travel. Or a couple hours, if you flew."

"I was thinking Vancouver."

"What do you know about Vancouver?"

"I don't know anything about Vancouver *or* Toronto."

"So what's the difference?"

"Two and a half thousand miles."

"Well, it's your call, Lee. But you've got a couple of weeks before anyone's going to be looking for you, and if I were in your shoes I'd want to poke around a bit before heading out, you know what I mean? Spit in the Grand Canyon? Go east, young man; it's Manifest Destiny in reverse." Robin touched the tip of the pencil to his temple. "Mental attitude." Standing, he said he was going to return to the business of harassing his father for money, but that he'd be back as soon as possible. After he left, Lee stood looking over the map. He'd only been to three states in his life, and one, Oregon, he'd driven through without getting out of his car. It occurred to him that if he did drive to New Jersey he could say goodbye to his family, strung out in a straightish line across the upper states: father in Washington, mother in Montana, sister Grace in New York. His brother Harry was in Minnesota; but Lee wouldn't visit Harry.

Minutes passed. Cal entered the kitchen wearing a bedsheet and a pair of outsize sunglasses. "Where's the Alka-Seltzer?" Lee said it was in the bathroom cupboard, and she padded away, returning a moment later with the Alka-Seltzer fizzing in a tooth glass. She sat at the table, took off her sunglasses, and cleaned the lenses on the sheet. She put the sunglasses back on. "Look, is there anything we need to talk about?"

"What do you mean?"

"I mean you're leaving, I'm staying, apparently."

"You're staying apparently."

"Yeah."

"Are you saying you want to come with me?"

"I don't know. I guess I'm not saying that, no."

"Then what's there to talk about?"

"Okay. Right." She sat still awhile. Lee thought possibly she was crying, but he couldn't be sure because of the sunglasses. "Are you crying?" he asked, and she answered that that was private information, and that she'd never tell, that Lee would never know—that he'd go to his grave not knowing. She drank the Alka-Seltzer and left the kitchen. Lee heard the groan of the mattress as she lay back down. He asked if she was okay and she called back, "I'm sad and shitty."

"But are you okay?"

"I guess so. You just tend to your business, Lee Clarke. I'll get out of your hair after a bit more sleep. Now please be quiet, all right?"

"All right."

Lee returned to his to-do list. He drew a line through *bus/plane/train?* Next on Lee's list was: *furniture.*

He had moved to California with practically nothing

in the way of furnishings, and for a time lived in his spacious one bedroom with only a mattress, a transistor radio, and a stack of apple crate bookshelves. One morning he was seduced by a commercial sales pitch he heard on the radio from an outfit called Bountiful Pacific Enterprises promising easy credit options for full-time students of accredited universities. He had never considered the words *no money down* before but now they were vibrational, and charged with secret meaning. He went into the Bountiful Pacific showroom telling himself he must be shrewd, he must exhibit worldliness, adultness—he needed a kitchen table and chairs, a portable record player, nothing more. But the salesman saw him for the mark he was and within forty-five minutes Lee had signed up for the Lifestyle Suite, a package including furnishings for each room of the apartment, a robust hi-fi system and television set, a full array of kitchen appliances, in addition to little niceties like sheets, pillowcases, towels, and cutlery. It was all delivered promptly and Lee's apartment was so radically transformed, and he was so affected by the transformation, that he felt he'd drunk the mythic American tonic. He was making the smallest allowable monthly payment so that the burden was easily manageable and was enjoying the merchandise to the utmost but six months later he received a loan summary, and in inspecting this document discovered he'd made virtually no progress against the principal and that at the current rate he wouldn't pay off the loan until the middle 1980s. In considering this far-off date he recognized that he'd been led astray, and his affections for the merchandise cooled. Now two years had passed, and the principal only slightly diminished, and the deterioration of the merchandise was uniform, the pots and pans scalded, towels worn, sheets pilled, and the sectional fraying at the arms. Sitting at the kitchen table, he asked himself what of the Lifestyle Suite he wished to take with him; the answer came that he wanted nothing, and he called the offices of Bountiful Pacific Enterprises to let them know about his imminent departure, and that they should come to collect their merchandise as soon as they were able. The company representative was alarmed. "It's going to be at least a week before we can get someone out your way."

"That's all right," said Lee. "I'll leave the key under the mat, your man comes when he comes."

"You miss my point."

"Okay, what is it?"

"It's that there needs to be an assessment made regards the wear and tear of the goods, and that you must be present for this process."

"Why?"

"The assessment will determine the updated terms of the loan."

"The updated terms of the loan," Lee said.

"Yes," said the representative. "You've decided you

want us to take the goods back. That's as may be, but the simple fact of your not possessing the goods does not absolve you of your debt. Now, if our man finds everything is shipshape, then we may agree to take it all back to resell in our secondhand showroom."

"Okay."

"But that's not a guarantee, and even if we do take it back, there will still be a balance owed. And then, if our man deems the merchandise unfit for return, you will owe us the full amount of the loan, whether or not the goods are in your possession."

"Why would I pay for all this stuff if I'm not going to keep it?"

"Those are the terms of the contract you put your name to."

"Right," said Lee. "Well, buddy, I'll tell you what. I'm leaving tomorrow morning, so you better come get your crap before the landlord hauls it all away."

"Now that you can't make the payments it's crap."

"It was crap before."

"Deadbeat."

"Come get your crap, creep."

"There goes your credit."

"There it goes."

"Deadbeat."

"Creep."

"Deadbeat."

Lee hung up the phone and drew a line through *furniture.* Cal said, "For someone who's supposed to be being quiet, you're being very loud."

"I'm sorry."

"Don't be sorry, be quiet."

"I could go see Mr. Headley."

"Be quiet!"

Lee stepped from the apartment and into the misty seaside morning, setting out on foot for Mr. Headley's repair shop. His coming to work for Mr. Headley was borne of the shop's proximity to his apartment, and his need to occasionally borrow tools. Mr. Headley was opposed to loaning tools but recognized in Lee a moral need to keep his machine well maintained, and so, as a fellow sufferer, and to his own surprise, he found himself making allowances for the sturdy young Washingtonian. After a period of months, Lee was allotted space to work in the yard behind the shop, and more than once was given use of the hydraulic lift. Lee offered money for such favors but Mr. Headley waved the thought away. The only point of contention between them stemmed from the fact of Mr. Headley's status as a Chevy man. And while he couldn't deny the time and care Lee put into his Ford, he couldn't help but disparage the brand whenever Lee walked up to meet him, sheepish in his needs:

"Fix or Repair Daily."

"First on Race Day."

"Found on the Road Dead."

"First on Race Day."

Mr. Headley liked Lee because Lee didn't speak unless there was something to say, and because the state of the Ford's engine evidenced an orderliness of Lee's heart. One day he said, "Look, do you want a job?"

"I'm in school, Mr. Headley."

"But you're not a student."

"Well, I am."

Mr. Headley shook his head. "You're a mechanic, kid. Let me know when you flunk out."

After the event of violence, Lee told him, "Okay, I flunked out. What's the pay?"

Mr. Headley took Lee on at $75 a week, a more-than-fair wage for thirty hours, enough to live comfortably, certainly; and now began a brief period of his life which, while absent any sort of direct adventure, was never dull, or ugly. On a given morning Lee might wake up alone, or with Cal, and as he made his coffee his mind would move in the direction of a half-finished job that waited for him, a Pontiac Parisienne in need of transmission repair, hoisted up on the lift. Making his way to the shop he would visualize the commencement of the day's labor, standing beneath the Pontiac's undercarriage, then climbing the stepladder, ascending into the cloud of the car's cold innards. During the hours of work he would be thinking of the coming evening, Cal in his kitchen, pointing at things with her cigarette, doing impressions of her professors, film actors, or herself, or Lee. They'd eat Chinese food, or spaghetti, then go to the movies, or into the city, to a club or bar. Some nights they would drive north on Highway 1, stopping at random, or not at all, driving to drive, speaking and not speaking, listening to the radio: Oxnard, Ventura, Santa Barbara, and back. Other nights, Lee would eat alone at a diner or a hot dog stand, then go home, with his books and records and television, a six-pack of beer. The days held a pleasurable shape, and Lee passed from one to the next with an easy heart. It was only later that this period of time revealed itself to be a sort of perfection, and which Lee would see too late was impossible to reconstruct.

The shop was obscured in the hazy mist; Mr. Headley met Lee at the door of the front office and beckoned for him to sit. Mr. Headley was not prone to joy but on this day he was pleased by what he believed was the story of the morning: Lee had been summoned to fight in the war in Vietnam and had elected to answer the call. Mr. Headley had favored Lee as an employee and now admired him as a citizen, and he produced a snapshot from his wallet, a picture of his days in the Marines, in Korea. The image featured a group of four soldiers standing shoulder to shoulder, each lively in the face, chattering. Mr. Headley set his dirty finger to the side of one of the faces. "Look at this, look—who might that young mischief maker be? Any one you've ever associated with?"

"That's you, Mr. Headley."

"Private Samuel Headley, reporting for duty—with not a care in the world or clear clue in his head. Well, the war gave him something to care about, as well as a clue or two to bring home with him." He named the other soldiers and described the specifics of their personalities, while Lee nodded and made little noises denoting interest. It was a rare instance of Lee feeling the need to act in a phony manner with Mr. Headley, and he wanted to get it over with. There was no part of him that wished to discuss his true feelings about being drafted with Mr. Headley, no piece of himself that thought it was possible, even, to bridge that gap. Mr. Headley's America was not the same as Lee's, and that was all. Mr. Headley was staring moonily at the picture of himself; he told Lee, "These are important times for you, kid. And they're going to keep being important. And I wish someone had told me that. You hear me?"

"Yeah."

"Pay close attention."

"Okay."

Mr. Headley gave Lee his wages, plus an extra twenty. "Go and have a ball with your girl. Remember this is hard for her too. I wish someone had told me *that*. There might have been someone waiting for me when I got home."

"Thanks, Mr. Headley."

"Don't thank me. What are you thanking me for? I should be thanking you!" He slapped Lee's back. "Hey, though, how'd your folks take it?"

"I haven't mentioned it to them yet."

Mr. Headley looked at Lee uncomprehendingly. "Son," he said. "You must tell your mother and father. And you must say your goodbyes to them. Because whether or not you're coming back home, nobody knows. Say your goodbyes without saying them, you know what I mean by that?"

"Yeah."

"Listen to Sam Headley. He was walking around and noticing things when you were still a glint in the old man's eye." He pulled out another bill, a crumpled five, and tucked it into Lee's shirt pocket. "For the garçon. Don't let him sit you next to the can." They shook hands and Lee walked back into the mist, a mask of garbage-scented moisture resting across his face. The smell of beach trash, which had been so off-putting to him when he first arrived, was something he would miss, he realized.

When Lee got back to the apartment Cal was asleep in his bed, her long blond hair obscuring her face, her bare shoulder exposed, and as he stood over her he understood this was the end of his knowing her in this way, and a sharp bitterness entered his heart. The smell of trash lingered in his nostrils and he went to the bathroom and got into the shower to rinse it away. The bitterness persisted and he sat down in the tub in a sulk of self-pity, the hot water drilling his skull and face. In a moment, Cal drew back the shower curtain. She was wearing panties and a bra and she asked, "What am I seeing?"

"Nothing. I'm tired. I'm unhappy about all this."

"You don't want to go?"

"Of course I don't want to go."

"Okay, but I didn't know that."

"You knew."

"Okay, but it's good to hear you say it."

"Do you want to get in with me?"

"Nothing personal, but no, I don't. You want some tea?"

Cal went away and Lee stood up and blew his nose and turned off the water and dried himself and combed his hair slickly back. He came into the kitchen wearing a towel and found Cal standing beside the table, dressed now, and her hair was up and she was reading Lee's list. She said, "You've done all the to-dos but me."

"Yeah."

"But what do you have to do before you draw the line through?"

"I don't know. Say goodbye, I guess."

She said, "You shouldn't treat a person as a chore to complete, Lee."

"Well, I don't think I am," he told her. Then: "You're not going to pick a fight with me, are you?"

"Why would I do that?"

"Because you're scared to say goodbye, and if we get into a fight you could storm off without having to do it?"

Cal thought about this. "That's just the kind of stunt I'd pull, isn't it?"

"Yeah." Lee crouched down and began unbuckling her shoes.

"What are you doing? I just put them on." But he didn't stop, and she didn't stop him. She patted his head. "You want the champagne now, or later?"

"Later." Slipping off her shoes, he rubbed her small, forever-cold feet. He led her by the hand back to bed. As they were making love the phone rang, then ceased ringing, then rang again, ceased again. After, Cal got up and went to the kitchen and returned with the half-empty bottle of champagne, which was of a low quality, and flat, and which they drank in bed, passing the bottle back and forth.

"Do you know what this party is?" asked Cal.

"What what party is?"

"This party we're having."

"What is it?"

"It's the Lee's Running-Away-from-America Party."

"Okay," said Lee.

Robin came into the apartment from the kitchen with a brown paper sack in his hand. He upended the sack, and cash slipped out onto the bed, five hundred dollars in tens and twenties. "Dad's a fascist, but he's my fascist." Next he produced a glassine baggie filled with white tablets and tossed it to Lee.

"What are these?" Lee asked.

"Those are bon voyage."

"But what are they?"

"White crosses, you know? Bennies. For driving."

"Driving pills."

"Yeah."

"How many do I take?"

"One or two or three or four or five."

"Depending on how well you want to drive," said Cal. She opened the baggie, picked one out, and ate it with the last swallow of champagne. "You don't even have a car," said Lee. Robin fetched the keys from Lee's pants then went out to the Ford, to sit in it and inspect it and live within the emotional reality of ownership. Cal got out of bed, bunched up her clothes, and moved to the bathroom. Robin returned with the pink slip and Lee signed over the Ford, using his knees as a table. Cal came out, dressed and ready for classes, hiding again behind her sunglasses.

Robin asked her, "What do you think of our boy, here?"

"What about him?"

"Dodge City."

"Yeah," said Cal. "Wasn't my idea." She looked at Lee a long time. "I'll be back later, okay?"

"Okay. What time?"

"I don't know. Later."

"What do you want to do tonight?"

"It doesn't matter. You decide." Lee watched her leave. She left the door open and Lee watched the open door. After she'd gone, Robin said, "Cal's cool."

"Yeah." Lee turned to Robin. "So I guess you're staying?"

"I guess I am."

"You going to go over there?"

"If the options are jail or Vietnam, I'll go to Vietnam."

"But those aren't the only options."

"I figure that's it for me."

"You wouldn't leave?"

"I don't think I would."

"Why not?"

"I just wouldn't do it."

"But why?"

"This is the place I live."

"That's not a reason."

"Sure it is. Look, I show up in Mexico, then what?"

"Figure it out when you get there."

"What's that mean?"

"It means figure it out. What about Canada?"

"Then what?"

"Figure it out."

"Yeah, it just seems like a fucked setup to me, Lee. I don't want to leave, you know? This is the country I grew up in, and I like it here, and my family's here, my friends. I know what things are like here, I'm comfortable here."

"Are you describing patriotism?"

"Maybe. I don't know. Am I? Who knows?"

"I think you are."

"I'm not not. Aren't you patriotic?"

"I've never thought about it before."

"I haven't either, but the draft presents us with a question."

"Don't you think it's a weird question to ask, though?"

"It's very weird."

"I think it's just too weird to take seriously. That's how I feel."

"Yeah."

"Maybe that makes me not a patriot."

"I think it does."

"Makes me not a patriot?"

"Yeah."

"But you're one, I guess."

"I'm not not."

"Why won't you say it outright?"

Robin was smiling. "What do you want from me, man?"

"Admit that you feel patriotic feelings."

Robin only shook his head. They both were smiling now, but Robin couldn't or wouldn't say the words. He left with the Ford and Lee got dressed and called the offices of the Four Winds Driveaway Company to say he was coming in. Stepping outside, he remembered he had no car. "Shit," he said. He took a bus, sitting in the back row and watching the heads all jounce and jiggle and bow in time.

The offices of Four Winds were dark and smelled of mold; Lee sat in a cramped cubicle with an amiable clerk who wore a sheen of grease across his forehead. "We've got you down as a stand-by on three separate jobs, Mr. Clarke. Have you decided which suits your fancy?"

"I'm thinking I'd take the car to New Jersey, if it's still available."

"It is, yes," answered the clerk. "Though that job is unique for certain reasons I can name now, if you don't mind." He pulled a file from a tall stack of files, opened and considered it. "The client, that is to say the owner of the car, is a regular of ours, and a particular man he is. We have delivered more than a dozen automobiles to him over the last several years, and while he has a usual West Coast driver, that fellow is unavailable just now. But we've told the client about your preliminary telephone interview, and he was intrigued by the fact of your seminarian studies. He asked that I should speak with you in person and use my own discretion. That's what happening here, now, do you understand?"

"Yes," said Lee.

"Yes," said the clerk. "Now, when I say that he's particular, I mean that he is cautious. And when I say he's cautious, I mean that he has reason to be."

"And what is the reason?"

"The man is keen to safeguard his property, Mr. Clarke. Which is understandable when I consider the cost of certain of the cars in his collection. The vehicle bound for New Jersey is worth more than a year of my salary, for God's sake. For goodness' sake. Excuse me."

It was here that Lee recalled what Robin had said about there being a plus and a minus with the job. The minus was the destination; what was the plus? Lee didn't know but couldn't ask. When the clerk suggested they go look at the car Lee said that that would be fine. The clerk led him to a fenced-in parking lot set behind the drive-away offices. The lot held six or seven unremarkable newish cars, and one brand-new Jaguar E-Type. It looked to have been just minted, the paint a rich British racing green, the nubs still on the tires. The clerk moved to stand beside it; he faced Lee and pointed at it. He opened the driver's-side door and welcomed Lee to sit, and Lee sat, and the musky leather sighed as it received him, the seat held him snugly in place as though it had been made to accommodate his dimensions. The steering wheel was lacquered wood, the odometer read 49 miles, and what Lee wanted more than anything was to make a long and thorough inspection of its engine under direct overhead lighting. But he understood it was best to hide his true feelings away, and he feigned polite interest as the clerk settled into the passenger seat and pointed out this and that feature of the automobile. Regarding the trip itself, the clerk told Lee, "The owner does not expect his drivers to dead head; but neither does he want them to sniff every flower blooming along the side of the road. Eight hours of sleep per night, but an equal eight, at minimum, of driving each day, and in an easterly direction—no egregious zigzags."

"I understand."

"On the phone you had the air of the looky-loo about you; but do you have any hard destinations in mind as you plot your course to New Jersey?"

"There's family on the way."

"Can we make the distinction between on the way and out of the way?"

"It's all in a line."

"Mom and Dad?"

"And sister."

"Not planning any lengthy stays, though, I'd hope?"

"No."

"Obviously we can't dictate where our drivers go once they're out of our sight, but you'll understand that we do like to know in advance if they've any grand schemes they're hoping to fit into the job at hand."

"I don't."

"Have you ever been arrested?"

"No."

"Have you any moving violations on record?"

"No."

"Do you use narcotics?"

"No."

"Drink alcohol to excess?"

"No."

"Is the motivation for your travel existential?"

"What?"

"The owner asked that I should ask that. I believe he sees a potential red flag in your taking time away from your studies. He is wary of questers at the helm of one of his cars, is the thing. Are you questing, Mr. Clarke?"

"I don't think that I am."

"You are not in the throes of a crisis of faith? You are not looking for big answers on the highways of the United States of America? The owner would rather not have his car be party to anyone's existential quest."

"I'm not questing."

"You don't *think* you are, you just said."

"I'm not."

"All right. That's fine. Now, I should like to discuss with you, if you don't mind, a uniquely curious aspect of my profession."

"I don't mind."

"Thank you." He extended and retracted his index finger. "On its surface, my job is a plain one. It is shipping, in effect. Goods transported from this to that point, in a timely fashion and with a minimum of fuss. But where my position differs from someone employed by, let's say, the US Postal Service, is that my company's success is reliant not on an interconnected team of salaried workers but on the *unpaid individual in lengthy isolation.* And it sometimes happens that such a man, absent witness and in control of a valuable piece of machinery, loses his sense of the ethical, the moral. Do you understand what I'm getting at?"

"I don't think that I do."

"Shall I explain further?"

"All right."

"A man pilots a fine automobile that is not his into and across a great expanse. Without the distractions of his life, the chatter of society, the blur of work, what happens? The man looks back. The man unburies. Perhaps he—laments. It is in this frame of mind that a certain type of person succumbs to a sense of indignation. And it has happened in the past that such a man, in such a state, becomes an unreliable steward of the vehicle entrusted to him. Cars have been used carelessly and damaged. Cars have been intentionally vandalized. Cars have been abandoned, even stolen. Now, I'm not saying this happens often, Mr. Clarke. Certainly I'm not saying I believe it will happen with you. But before I could consider passing the keys to a car like this over to you it's important that you know such a phenomenon exists. Let's call it a cautionary tale and be done with it, yes?"

"Yes."

"Fine. Now, I feel that I know people, and I'm looking at you and I believe that I can trust you to see this job through. What do you think about that?"

"I think that's very nice."

"But do you feel that you can see the job through?"

"Yes."

"Well, I'm satisfied. Do you have any questions? No? Shall we get started on the paperwork?" Lee followed the clerk back into the offices, and they sat again in the too-small cubicle, and Lee signed his name many several times. After this he was given the keys, and the clerk shook his hand, and three minutes later Lee was in possession of a car he'd have been thrilled to see simply driving past. He pulled from the lot and drove a quarter mile, slowly, stopping at the first gas station he saw. He parked at the pump and opened the hood to make his study of the engine.

Lee thought of the Devonian period, of the first fish-like being flinging itself from the muck and onto the shore, that initial suicidal spasm toward the ambulatory reality of humanness. Later, distant relatives of this same creature came together to design and fabricate the Jaguar's engine, the sight of which summoned a glad fascination in Lee, and he was pleased that he should be alive at this present moment in mankind's history.

To be in possession of the Jaguar offset Lee's sense of disaster; as he made his way home, trying out the car for speed and handling on the Harbor Freeway, he decided he would take Cal out for a fancy dinner in Santa Monica, and after make one final run to Santa Barbara and back—a stylish farewell and fitting end, and Lee was soothed at the thought of it, but the plan was dashed when he got home and found a note bubble-gummed to his front door:

I can't do the big goodbye scene, Lee. I love you basically but I can't do it and I'm sorry, seriously. I'm my mother's daughter, and she taught me that all emotion must be ground to a powder and tossed down the well, so that's my method for dealing with your leaving. Will you call me from the road? You can yell at me, then forgive me? Or not yell at all, and the forgiveness will just come about magically, the way it sometimes does?

—Calliope.

Lee poked at the bubble gum; still soft. He loaded his suitcase into the backseat of the Jaguar, took a white cross with a palmful of tap water, and drove to the ocean, heading north on the Pacific Coast Highway.

MELTING PARADE MUSIC

LEE HAD BEEN DRIVING AT SPEED FOR LONG NIGHT hours along the winding coastal roads of Southern and then Central California. His blood simmered with stimulant narcotics and as the miles peeled off he became hypnotized by his own motion, the redundancy of visual information—the Jaguar's high beams bending into curve after hard curve, cones of light chasing after the unspooling white line in the center of the road. At times Lee experienced a sense of pure and total control over the Jaguar, that the machinery was functioning as an extension of his wordless desires; at other times he felt his role was passive, that the car was operating itself, as if the chassis were locked into a track. He drove with the windows down, the cold, salty wind numbing his face and hands, the radio coming in and out of focus as he passed through this and that town. South of Morro Bay he came across a night-owl DJ on an opera jag, and turned it up as loud as he might. When the station dropped to static, Lee listened to this. It sounded like grease frying, and his empty stomach burbled and he became nauseated and shut the radio off, listening then to the wind in his ears, the ocean toiling in the vast blackness to his left. He rolled up the window and listened to the muffled engine—a thoughtful growling when he downshifted, as though it were making a concession, its optimistic rallying when he upshifted. The Benzedrine pushed him along, his mind untroubled by his attendant problems, but bright with the sense he might at any moment have an idea of majestic significance.

He stopped for gas at a nameless turnout in between Cambria and San Simeon; across the road from the gas station was an all-night diner. Lee couldn't consider eating, but his shirt was damp with sweat, his hands cramped from gripping the wheel, and he wanted to have a drink and generally unclench himself. The diner was called Ed & Eddie's and was a lively little dive with tabletop jukeboxes in each of the five horseshoe booths, these overfilled with a crowd of teenaged boys and girls who had adopted the place as their clubhouse—jolly and loud and without worldly concern. Lee sat at the counter and ordered a beer, making his secret study of the group. In two or three years, certain of the young men might find themselves in a similar position to his own; but for now they were eating off one another's plates and talking or trying to talk to the girls, their voices rising up as they made attempts at wit and humor. The girls talked mainly to one another, and their voices were low, sharing nonhumorous confidences. Some among the boys became fascinated by the idea that they might play the same song on each jukebox at the same time, and Lee listened in on the chatter as a ringleader went from table to table discussing the plan and pooling change in anticipation of its realization. Lee enjoyed the teenagers but also felt a vague envy at the simplicity of their existence, and he turned away and into himself to brood. He drank his beer and ordered another, stepping away before it arrived and shutting himself up in a phone booth to call Cal, though it was the middle of the night. It rang twenty times and he hung up and exited the phone booth and went to stand before the mirror in the restroom. His flesh was clammy, his pupils full and inky. He washed his face and returned to the counter and drank his beer and resumed his consideration of the teenagers. The jukebox scheme was on the cusp of realization: the ringleader stood in readiness before his friends, his hands poised, pointing at the ceiling. He counted off an even three and the jukeboxes each were triggered, each playing the same song, a Sousa-style parade march.

The fact of the song being played five times at once lent the already bombastic tune an epic stature, and through the first verse and chorus, all in the room were fixated by pleasure and impressiveness, the waitress pausing to take it in, and the cook standing in the open door of the kitchen in his smock, clanging two spatulas together to show that he approved. But then at the midpoint of the second verse, and with the jukeboxes running at slightly odd tempos, there followed a slow coming apart of the melody, so that by the time the second chorus came around the song had devolved and now was melted, warped. The teenagers found this comical; they made melted, warping faces at one another, but Lee sensed something displeasing, even worrying in the song's unraveling. He put a dollar bill under his glass of beer and left the diner, eager to return to the purposeful northbound coastal Jaguar mindset, but the drugs had begun their abatement, and with them went his sureness of purpose, and he was reminded that the American military had stolen his life away, that Cal had utilized bubble gum to sever ties with him, and that Canada might as well be another planet. A black mood settled into the basin of

Lee Clarke's mind, and his stomach burned with an acid tanginess as he drove with miserable determination up-coast, a milky seaside moon replaced by the dull glow of dawn's first light within which it was revealed that every single thing that could be spoiled was spoiled.

THE MENDOCINO HOTEL

LEE PULLED OFF AT MENDOCINO, LOOPED THE LITTLE town twice and parked in front of the old Mendocino Hotel, gingham curtains bunched in its windows, the flat clapboard facade and wooden sidewalk recalling the middle nineteenth century. The Jaguar clicked and breathed and ticked; when Lee got out of the car the wind coming in off the ocean nearly knocked him over, the waves churning in the bay. He took up his suitcase and made for the lobby, crossing the carpeted foyer and to the glassed-in front desk where the manager sat looking out at the world.

"Good morning, how are you?" said Lee.

"I am in my cage," the manager answered. This was spoken in a way that Lee took to mean: all was proceeding to plan. Lee asked after a room and the manager said he could have one ready in fifteen minutes. Lee asked about a pay phone and the manager pointed a hooked finger. "Around the corner. Coffee too, help yourself." He stood and turned and disappeared into his sanctum. Lee sought out the coffee urn and poured himself a paper cupful. There was an old man sitting on a bench beside the urn; his somber clothing matched the room's wallpaper and furnishings so that he and the room looked to belong together. A sign hung crookedly from a nail on the wall: COFFEE FOR GUESTS ONLY!!! As Lee stirred in his sugar and powdered creamer, he sensed the old man's eyes on him. He didn't turn to look, because he didn't want to talk to anyone, but a moment later the old man asked Lee if he was checking in, and Lee nodded.

"Where you headed?"

"New Jersey."

"Where you coming from?"

"Los Angeles."

"You're going in the wrong direction, fellow." The old man pointed east, over his shoulder.

"I'll get there," said Lee.

"Sooner or later," the old man said.

Lee shut himself into a phone booth and called Cal

but she didn't answer. He called his father in Concrete but he didn't answer. He called his mother in Billings but she didn't answer. He called his sister Grace in Manhattan, who picked up on the first ring and said, "Yes, what?"

"Is that how they say good morning in New York?"

"Lee?"

"Yeah."

"What are you doing?"

"Telephoning. What's the matter?"

"I'm mad."

"You sound mad. What happened?"

"It's a whole big story. Why are you calling so early?"

"I've been up all night. Tell me the story."

"Okay, hold on." Lee heard Grace light a cigarette. She said, "I got myself into a situation with my superior at the hospital. Maybe you're familiar with the torrid particulars; it fits in with any daytime soap opera. Here's a hint: I'm the impressionable small-town nurse-in-training."

"He's the handsome young doctor?"

"Not that handsome."

"Young?"

"Not that young."

"Beloved by colleagues and patients alike?"

"Not really, no."

"Married to his work?"

"That he is. Also, though, he's married to his wife.

Our lady of the persistent mustache. Who recently learned about the impressionable small-town nurse-in-training."

"How'd she find out?"

"I rang her up and told her all about it."

"Grace Lynne Clarke."

"Yeah, buddy. I've never really hated someone before now, and I'll tell you what it's not, it's not boring."

"You sound all puffed up."

"I'm very puffed up."

"And this is happening right now?"

"It's two days old."

"Where's it at?"

"After the initial flurry of violence, we've arrived at eerie silence."

"Where's the good doctor?"

"Called in sick."

"Wrote himself a note."

"Right. I think he's terrified."

"Of you or the wife?"

"Me."

"Was there a not-bad part before the bad?"

"The last six months were as not-bad as could be."

"Spring fling?"

"Winter into spring."

"And now the fling's come to an end?"

"Not if I have anything to say about it."

"You're going to get yourself fired."

"I'd like to see him try to get me fired, boy. I'd genuinely like to see it."

"What'll you do if he does?"

"Make a shrill noise. There were behaviors, Leland. Closed-door behaviors his superiors would be shocked to hear about."

"I don't know if I want to know."

"I don't know if you do."

"And since when are you such a shit disturber?"

"Since the good doctor."

"Where do you see it all going?"

Grace took a draw on her cigarette. "There's no way to cut it that it doesn't end in corpses."

"Wow," said Lee. Then, politely: "How's school?"

"It's fine."

"School's fine?"

"That's right. I mean, I'm making my grades, but something's changed, it's true. I guess my big epiphany is that I may or may not become a nurse, but that I will definitely continue to live in New York City."

"You were so gung ho to help people."

"I don't not want to help them now. It's just that I'd rather sit around having fascinating conversations."

"You've been corrupted, sounds like."

"I have been absolutely and totally corrupted, yes."

"How's it feel?"

"Well, I'm in agony at the moment. But I'm invested

and interested in my life in a way that's totally alien to what came before. I wouldn't trade places with anyone for anything, is the truth of it."

The operator came on and asked for more money. Lee dropped a half dozen dimes down the pay phone's coin slot and the operator went away.

Grace asked, "Sorry, where are you? And why haven't you slept?"

"I'm in Mendocino, and I haven't slept because I've been driving all night to get here."

"And how does one drive all night to Mendocino without sleeping?"

"One takes these little white pills."

"And why does one do it?"

"You're not the only person with a whole big story."

"Tell it," she told him, and Lee explained about his getting kicked out of school, the draft notice, the drive-away car to New Jersey. Grace's voice had dropped. "I'm listening so hard right now."

"Well, that's all of it."

"And you're not going to go, is that the idea?"

"To Vietnam? No, I'm not going to go."

"You're going to go to Canada?"

"Yeah."

"Who do you know in Canada?"

"I don't know a soul in Canada."

"Fuck, Lee."

"Tell me about it."

"Are you all right?"

"Not all right."

"Things were good in LA?"

"I was happy, yeah."

"What about your gal, she coming along?"

"Cal, yeah, no, she's not."

"Well," said Grace, "if you're driving to Jersey then I propose you take a little detour, come visit your big sister."

"That's what I was thinking."

"You'll stay a couple days?"

"Sure."

"I could cheer you up."

"You could try."

"You going to see Mom and Dad?"

"I think I should, yeah."

"What about Harry?"

"Fuck Harry."

"You're going to have to forgive him sooner or later."

"Not true."

"When are you going to see Dad?"

"Depends on how long I sleep, but I'll get to Concrete tomorrow, sometime. When was the last time you were in touch? He's not picking up his phone much these days."

"Oh, I gave up on Dad last year."

"Nothing from him?"

"He doesn't answer my letters."

"I wonder how he's doing."

"You can fill me in tomorrow."

"Yeah."

"Did I tell you Mom's mad at me?"

"You didn't, no. Why?"

"I let her know about the good doctor."

"You're telling everyone everything."

"I've entered my verbal period. Mom's position, and it's a compelling one, is not so much that I'm in the wrong morally but that I'm giving too much of myself away to a shabby man."

"You told her he's shabby?"

"She decided he must be."

"Okay but is he?"

"Shabby? I guess he is, after all's said and done. Mom told me I'm going to be embarrassed later to've cared in the first place, and I could sense on the level of the subconscious that she was right. Doesn't do me much good now, but there you are." She took another draw of her cigarette. "So you're a doper and I'm a home-wrecker."

"The pride of Concrete."

"Will you call me from Dad's?"

"Sure."

Lee was startled by a knock on the glass door of the telephone booth. The old man stood waiting for him; Lee opened the door. "Yes, what?"

"You heading back out in the morning?"

"I don't know. I'm talking on the telephone."

"Because there's a storm landing about suppertime tonight. It'll probably bring down a few trees across the roads."

"I'm talking on the telephone."

"Okay but what I'm saying to you is, if I were you I'd head out before, or plan on staying another day, maybe two."

Lee closed the door on the old man, who asked through the glass, "You think I'm fooling around?" Over the old man's shoulder, Lee saw the manager come around the corner. The moment the manager noticed the old man, his face darkened and he began clapping his hands, as if to shoo a crow. "Out, out!" he said. The old man was not surprised or offended; he pivoted and aimed himself at the exit and made his way across the foyer. The manager stared after the old man awhile, then turned to Lee, held up a key, and made a show of setting it beside the coffee urn. Lee nodded that he understood and the manager walked away and Lee returned to the phone to tell Grace his room was ready but she had hung up, or the phone call had timed out. He climbed the creaking stairs to his room, showered, and dropped into bed. The wind coming off the sea rattled the windows in their jambs and his sleep was plagued by dreams of insignificant frustrations: a doorknob turning endlessly, a train stuck in the station. He woke up at 5 p.m. to the sound of an air-raid siren bellowing at the town. He called the front desk to ask what it meant in terms of his leaving and the manager said that he probably shouldn't leave at all, but that if he was going to chance it, now was the time. Lee dressed and took a white cross and soon was sitting in the Jaguar, warming the engine and listening to the emergency warnings on the radio. He drove around the town; there was not a soul out walking, and all the shops were closed. The sky was meanly dark, and Lee slowed as he drove by the towering air-raid siren, still droning on. He was impressed by the dimensions of its noise; it overpowered every other consideration, and he sensed its weight bearing down on him as he passed underneath it.

He drove a dozen miles upcoast on Highway 1, the wind pushing in off the ocean and bullying the Jaguar back and forth across the center line, the rain coming down in tilting sheets. South of Fort Bragg he came to a turnoff for a minor eastbound highway that would connect him to the 101 and he decided it was time to say goodbye to the West Coast of North America. A patrolman was parked at the highway's entrance; he flashed his lights at Lee and Lee pulled over. The patrolman exited the car and dashed in a hunch to Lee's driver's-side window. He wore a shiny black slicker, his face was large and red and wet and he had to yell to make himself heard over the wind: "Where do you think you're going?"

"East."

"You don't want to go in there. There's not a straightaway for forty miles, spaghetti all the way to Willits."

"I need to get to the 101."

The patrolman shook his head. "Some of those big boys are coming down. Probably some of them already have. And if you think anyone's going to trek in there to pull you out before the storm's through then I've got some bad news."

Lee asked, "Are you telling me the road's closed?"

"I'm not telling you that."

Lee said, "Sir, I'm driving on."

The patrolman looked at Lee for a silent moment, then stood up straight, stepped back, and made an after-you gesture.

Lee entered the dark mouth of the redwood forest moving slowly, as one stepping into a cathedral, looking up and around, taking in the chasmic dimensions of the great room. The somber radio voices continued their warnings that it was time to find shelter. The wind was absurd, the trees swaying and bowing; branches and boughs dropped from the sky and were strewn across the pavement. The Jaguar swerved nimbly around this and that obstacle and Lee's speed increased with each quarter mile. The narcotics had taken hold and had again ushered him to the place of momentary superconfidence; it soon became apparent to him that he was destined to take the highway to Willits as fast as he was able. It seemed the Jaguar was made for just such a trial as this and there was for Lee a flawless sense of immaculate order as he plummeted into hairpins, and up out of deep gullies. Twenty miles of concentrated and important-feeling driving had occurred when Lee came around a long, right-bending turn to find a midsize redwood fallen fully across the highway. He drew the Jaguar to a short stop and sat idling, panting and staring at the tree, feeling for some moments a sense of indignity. But that the highway was cut into an incline meant that the tree was not lying flat on the pavement but rested at an angle, and with a gap separating its trunk from the left-hand lane of the road. Lee got out of the car; he measured the top of the Jaguar at chest height, then approached the tree to check this against the height of the gap. The churned-up earth still was fresh at the redwood's root; Lee could smell it on the air—it must have only just fallen, and so he was wary of it settling. But he measured the gap and there was, he believed, room enough to clear the Jaguar. Walking back to the car, cutting through the noise of the storm, he heard the sound of a tree snapping in the far distance; carnage made quaint by the fact of its remove. He sat awhile in the idling Jaguar. He drove forward in first gear and the car crept under the redwood with inches to spare. Reaching up and out the window, Lee Clarke touched the tips of his fingers to the bark of the tree.

CONCRETE

LEE APPROACHED THE TOWN OF CONCRETE AT EIGHT o'clock in the morning absent any sense of nostalgia or unhappiness but taking stock in the general sense, as one returning to his origins must always take stock. The details of his childhood and young adulthood were much like that of his peers: he and his sister and brother and father and mother living together under the one roof, his father a twenty-year factory man, his mother a part-time clerk at the post office. It was elementary school with light mischief, Christmases, birthdays, cowboys and Indians. High school brought elevated stakes for Lee: fights with the local boys and the boys in the neighboring towns, the comforts of male comradeship, the alien joy of romantic fascination. It had all felt significant enough to Lee until he left Concrete and stood before the Pacific Ocean, the sight of which illustrated his trifling stature, and that his experience was common to the point of plainness.

Other than Lee's falling-out with his brother Harry, the only true drama of his life in Concrete came at the start of his senior year of high school, when his mother and father abruptly divorced. He and his siblings had taken it for granted that their parents would see the union through to the grave, but then came the morning when their father was making them breakfast, which had never happened before. "Your mother isn't feeling well," he said, but he wore a tragic countenance that implied a truth obscured. The next morning his mother was back at the stove, but her gaze was remote, and she had no answers other than to say she was fine, yes, better. The morning after this Lee watched his mother walking down the front path with a suitcase in each hand and toward a taxi idling in the road. She'd left a letter for her children with the neighbor, Mrs. Whitman; the old woman had put the envelope in Lee's hand after Lee's father had gone to work. The first line read: *This is an apology and an explanation.* The last line: *I truly believed I could wait until you three were gone and settled into your lives, but my strength flagged, and I hope, I sorely hope you'll forgive me my eleventh-hour weakness.* She moved back to her hometown of Billings, Montana, and was living with her brother Wallace in the house they'd grown up in. She maintained frequent contact with each of her children, long letters and phone calls, gift packages, requests for visitors. She was adamant that Lee should go to college, advised him on his major, and rewrote his admissions essay from top to bottom. Lee's grades were respectable; but as the admissions officer himself said in the acceptance letter, it was the insights offered by the essay that clinched his position.

Lee was not angry at his mother for leaving, but he hadn't understood it; after he left for California he asked why she'd gone away like that and she thought a moment and explained, "There is love and there is not love." One doesn't typically consider the social value of a parent outside of their parental role; one doesn't think of who they truly are. But Lee's mother's answer forced Lee to look at his father as a man, a human being.

Lee's father was never at the front of the pack in his peer group, never pronounced in his behaviors one way or the other: he worked at work-time and fished at fishing-time and drank beer at beer-drinking-time. In the wake of his wife's abandonment, however, the cord connecting him to his duties was severed, his devolution commenced, and the siblings were taken up with a group repulsion that begat in each of them a need to bolt. Harry, the eldest, moved almost at once, finding work at a steel mill in Duluth. Grace, Lee's twin sister, had landed a scholarship in the psychology department at Barnard with an attached internship at Bellevue among the variously insane. She headed east months before the semester began, claiming a desire to acclimate to the city, but Lee knew, and she knew Lee knew, that her true motivation was to get away. By the time Lee left for California his father had been fired from the concrete factory, his drinking was on to the next level, the story set in motion. And while it was true that Lee had never admired his father, he had always liked him; he understood as he drove away in the Ford that he was abandoning a decent man at his time of need.

Across Lee's two years in California, their contact was unrobust: occasional letters which gave way to postcards, and then the odd abbreviated phone call on this or that birthday or holiday. Lee never pushed for answers to questions relating to the daily reality of his father's life, partly because his father obviously didn't care to share, but also because Lee suspected the answers would be dire, and that if he were granted access to the truth he would be expected or impelled to do something about it. His father was friendly on the phone in a way that felt performative, which was fatiguing to sit through and must surely have been as or more fatiguing to embody. They'd not been in touch in five months and now, as Lee drew closer to the town and man, he doubted his own sincerity in wishing to see his father at all. Some part of Lee's heart implored him to push on, to pass the town by, and for the phase of miles preceding the turnoff he felt it likely he would not stop. But his stomach was a pit of heat, his nerves raw from the ebbing stimulants, and he wanted to shower, eat, sleep; at the half-mile signpost his foot came away from the gas, and he downshifted and pulled off the highway. Soon he was driving the Jaguar through and around the town, looking at this and that physical or emotional landmark but making generally for the house he'd lived in up to his eighteenth year.

Concrete looked shabbier than before. Half the storefronts were boarded up and dandelions grew in the cracks of the sidewalks. Lee parked across the street from his house and climbed out of the Jaguar, stretching his back and legs and making a study of the property. When Lee was growing up it had always been tidy and well maintained; now the lawn was overgrown, moss clung to the edges of the roof, and a rusted refrigerator rested on its side where the sidewalk met the gate. There was a white panel van parked crookedly in the dirt driveway; as Lee crossed the road he saw that it was a dogcatcher's van, and that there was a man in the cab. Stepping closer, he realized that the man was his father. He wore white pants and a white coat and there were dirty bandages on his hands and fingers and he was sleeping sitting up, his arms crossed. Lee knocked on the window and his father blinked and turned.

"Leland, good morning, what in the world?"

"Hi, Dad," said Lee. Not knowing what else to say, he asked, "How are you?"

"Okay, thanks. How are you?"

"I'm all right. I was going by, you know."

"Thought you'd check on the old man?"

"That's right."

"Fine by me. You planning to stay long?"

"No, I'm on my way somewhere. I thought I might clean up and rest a bit if that's all right."

"Of course it's all right." He pointed at Lee's wrist. "What time is it?"

"Eight-thirty."

"Oh, boy! I better get ready for work. You want a cup of coffee?"

"That'd be good. I'm pretty hungry, too."

"Well, let's just take a look and see what can be done." Lee's father exited the panel van and walked up the path to the front door. When he put his key in the lock there came from within the house the sound of many barking dogs. "Mind your hands," he said. He opened the door and entered the house with an attitude of vigor and thrust, pulling Lee in after him. There were twenty or more dogs of various ages, sizes, and breeds moving freely around the house. They did not give off any uniform emotional opinion; some were barking madly while others were docile, affection-seeking; others still were frightened and hid themselves away in corners and under the kitchen table.

Lee's father passed through the body of these animals as one fording a river, his bandaged hands held up under his chin in a demure gesture of safeguard. Certain of the dogs did seem to dislike him strongly, lunging and nipping at him. He crossed the living room and opened the sliding glass doors, the dogs pouring out of the house and into the backyard. He closed the doors and breathed a moment, basking in the relative peace before shuffling into the kitchen, searching for something to feed his son. He opened and shut this and that drawer and cabinet; shaking his head, he said, "No, there doesn't seem to be much in stock at the moment. But how about this: why don't you put on some water for coffee while I have myself a little birdbath. After that I'll make an appearance at work, then we can hit the diner, full spread, my treat, what do you think?" Lee agreed that that sounded fine, and his father went away to the bathroom. In a moment there came the sound of running water, followed by a muted retching, a toilet flushing. Lee put the kettle on before making an inspection of the kitchen: chaos and grime, the face of the oven blackened by fire, its handle melted down in a low, fixed droop. Some drawers held bundles of unopened mail, some empty bourbon bottles, some dog collars. The sink was overfilled with dirty dishes and Lee had to root around for a pair of mugs, and both needed thorough washing. The kettle rose to a boil; Lee discovered there was no sugar or milk and that the coffee tin was empty. The only consumable product he could find besides salt and pepper was a two-thirds-empty fifth of Ten High, which he set in the center of the kitchen table.

Lee's father returned, clean-shaven, hair combed back, fresh bandages on his hands. He eased himself into his chair as one in manageable pain, holding his hands on his lap, out of sight, but a tremor ran up the arms and jostled him at the shoulder. His flesh held a gray cast, and there was a coagulating blob of blood on his cheek beneath his right eye. Lee pointed. "You've got some blood." Lee's father touched the blob with a trembling index finger. He studied the blood, rubbing it thoughtfully with his thumb. Now he noticed the bourbon bottle on the table, which brought a pucker of discomfort to his face.

"Where's the coffee?" he asked.

"All out."

"What's that doing there?"

"Well, you've got the shakes and I've been up all night driving and we can eat later but for now I think we should both have a drink, all right?"

Lee's father said, "I don't like to take a drink before the sun goes down."

"Yeah," said Lee. "I don't think that's particularly true, Dad. Anyway, I'm going to have one, and I'd appreciate it if you joined me." Lee poured out two long shots into the coffee cups and set them on the table.

"You first," said Lee's father, and Lee drank, then his

father drank, and after sat swallowing and reswallowing, tasting and retasting the bourbon. His eyes were closed and he was breathing through his nose.

"You want another?" Lee asked.

"Not yet."

"What happened to the oven?"

"Burnt up a chicken." Lee's father opened his eyes. "Wait one minute. Why aren't you in school?"

"I was kicked out."

"Why'd you get kicked out?"

"I got into a fight on campus."

"Who with?"

"Another student."

"You win the fight?"

"Wasn't much of a fight."

"One-punch wonder?"

"Yeah."

"Knocked him down on the ground?"

"Yeah."

"To his knees or flat out?"

"Flat out."

"*He* get kicked out of school?"

"No."

"So what's the lesson learned?"

"I don't really know."

Lee's father looked away, out the kitchen window and at the Jaguar across the street. "What about the car?"

"What about it?"

"It's a little nifty, isn't it?"

"Sure it's nifty. It's a drive-away."

"Where you driving it away to?"

"New Jersey. I'll say this, it moves right along. You want to take a ride?"

Lee's father stared. "I'm not going around in that thing."

"Why not?"

"I have to live here, Lee. Anyway, I got to get to the pound. I'm a dogcatcher now."

"I gathered that."

"You want to come along with me on my rounds? I'll let you honk the horn. It's take-your-son-to-work day." Lee's father rose from the table and returned to open the sliding glass doors. As the dogs streamed back into the house he asked the pack of them, "Who's ready for the big show?" He picked out a little mutt with wiry gray hair, tucked the dog under his arm like a football and beckoned for Lee to follow him out to the panel van. "Careful you don't let any of these buddies out," he advised. The cab of the panel van was thick with the moldering scents of Lee's father's vapors. Lee rolled down the window and breathed the cool morning air of Washington state. He said, "Interesting times for you, Dad."

Lee's father didn't respond.

"How'd it happen?"

"What part?"

"The dogcatcher part."

"Last job in town. I needed something to do." He shrugged, took up the CB from its holster on the face of the dashboard. "Keep quiet while I call in to Big Cap, will you?" In a cheerful tone he said, "Big Cap, you there? Big Cap, come back."

A deep voice, joyless, issued from the plastic handset: "Clarke."

"Clarke here. What's passing for news on your side, Cap?"

"I was just sitting around wondering if you were going to make it to work on time or not. I thought probably not."

"Think again, Cap. I just made my morning rounds, and I already got one in the can."

"What?"

"I said I already got one in the can."

"Huh," said Big Cap.

"I'll be by for drop-off. You want me to bring you a coffee or doughnut or anything?"

"No, I don't."

"Okay then, I'll see you."

The line went dead and Lee's father hung up his CB. "Big Cap's what you'd call a tough nut," he told Lee. "Doesn't like anything about being alive, so far as I can tell. And I've tried it every which way, but the truth is that he's just a terrible old guy. Also, I think he's on to my little scheme."

"What scheme is that?"

"Well, don't you find it odd, Lee, that the house is full up with dogs?"

"Yeah, Dad, I do."

"And what do you think's going on, there?"

Somehow it hadn't occurred to Lee to try to make sense of the situation; but suddenly he understood. "You're stealing those dogs, aren't you?"

"Correct."

"Why?"

"Because there's a quota, which, if I don't meet it, I'll be fired. And there's no meeting it unless I bring in my own dogs."

"What's the quota?"

"Dog a day keeps me on the payroll. Two dogs and Big Cap gives me the afternoon off. When things get really bad I bring in three."

"Where are you getting the dogs?"

"Oh, here and there. Sedro-Woolley, mainly."

"But how do you do it?"

"I drive over nights, tool around. If I see a yard with a doghouse, I sneak up to the fence and wag some raw skirt steak around. It's not hard," he said assuredly, as if the idea of its difficulty might be the source of Lee's concern. They set out for the pound, Lee looking out one window, his father out the other, the wiry mutt curled up and sleeping between them. Lee's father operated the vehicle at around fifteen miles an hour.

"How's the old stomping ground look to you, son?"

"Pretty run-down."

"Does it?"

"Yeah."

"The boys are off to Vietnam. My pals, the first-stringers, most of them are dying or dead. And young people aren't getting married anymore, nobody's having babies, and nobody's moving here to take the dead folks' place. So that's the state of things. Some towns live and some don't."

They parked out front of a single-story brick building. Stencil-painted on the front door were the words ANIMAL CONTROL. Lee's father pulled a half-empty glass flask from underneath his seat and took a powerful drink of bourbon, chasing this with a breath mint, which he chewed up and swallowed. He picked up the dog and said, "Five minutes, right?" Lee watched his father climb the steps to enter the building and after sat naming all the reasons he shouldn't have come. The uplift from the Benzedrine was completely gone now, replaced by a leaden tiredness, and with a natural sorrow embroidering its edges. He performed an inspection of the van, unsurprised by the empties and trash stuffed under the seat but puzzled by the glove box, filled as it was with snacks and cigarettes and aspirin and Pepto-Bismol, the products all stacked neatly, labels facing outward, as if on display for purchase. Ten minutes passed and Lee's father exited the pound, dogless and dark in the face. As he climbed into the cab he said, "Okay, he's definitely on to me."

"What'd he say?"

"He's just staring all sideways and mean, but smiling, too, like he's going to nail me and that he's looking forward to it. Good Lord, what comes next?" He reversed the van and pulled onto the road. "I understand the desire to be boss," he said. "That part's always made sense to me. The part that *doesn't* make sense is, why is it that the bastard always gets there first?"

"Maybe it's that he wants it more than the others do."

"A sound theory, and likely true." Again he was topping off at about fifteen miles an hour. "You still hungry?"

"We haven't eaten."

"You still want to go to the diner?"

"So that we can eat, yeah."

"You're testy, Lee."

The diner was all but empty and they settled into a booth. A waitress came along and Lee ordered bacon and eggs and toast and potatoes, while Lee's father claimed to be unhungry.

"You're not going to eat anything?" Lee asked.

"He never does eat much," the waitress told Lee.

"Maybe you should eat just a little something."

"I always tell him he ought to," said the waitress. "You've *got* to eat or else then what?"

"I could go for an egg," Lee's father said.

"Is he telling me he wants one egg?" the waitress asked Lee.

"Hard-boiled egg and white toast," said Lee's father.

After the waitress went away, Lee's father drank half his coffee in a gulp and filled up the remainder with the glass flask of bourbon. As he sipped at this concoction he became ever more present, the bourbon sobering him, filling him out dimensionally. Their food arrived and Lee's father nibbled contentedly at the crusts of his toast. He was sitting upright and looking Lee in the eye; now he wished to talk.

"Well, son," he said, "how is everybody?"

"Fine, I guess."

"Don't just say 'fine.' How are they? How's your sister?"

"She's good. She's all right."

"Which is it, good or all right?"

"She's all right. I think she's going through some social confusions."

"What's that mean?"

"Beau problems."

Lee's father's shook his head. "Not my domain."

Lee thought about Grace navigating the tidal crowds across the broad avenues of the city. "I can't imagine her in Manhattan," he said.

"What do you know about Manhattan?"

"Nothing."

"What about the lunatics?"

"What about them?"

"Why is she there with them?"

"It's what she's studying."

"Lunatics."

"It's her interest." Lee shrugged. "You could ask her about it anytime you want to, you know."

"She doesn't want to talk to me."

"Sure she does."

"She said that?"

"She always asks how you are."

"And what do you say?"

"I used to say I thought you were fine; now I say I don't know, because I don't, because you never pick up the phone or answer my letters anymore."

Lee's father took a dainty bite of his hard-boiled egg. "And next time she asks, then what?"

"What do you want me to tell her?"

"Whatever you think is the truth."

Lee said, "You can go ahead and tell me what the truth is now, Dad, if you think I'm missing it, or likely to miss it later."

"No, you just go ahead and say what you say. It doesn't matter very much, I don't think. What about your brother?"

"You know Harry and I don't talk."

"I did not know that. Since when don't you talk?"

"Since the eleventh grade."

Lee's father wagged his finger. "Are you still mad at him for screwing your girlfriend?"

"She wasn't my girlfriend."

"Wasn't she some terrific Communist tart?"

"Not at all."

"And you haven't talked to Harry in all this time?"

"No."

"He's your brother, Lee."

"We've never gotten along."

Lee's father sat remembering. "You never did, did you? Why is that?"

"I think it's his personality."

"Or yours."

"It's his."

Lee's father nodded that he understood. "He called me week before last sniffing around for 'a loan.' I'm putting that in quotes. 'A loan.'"

"Did you give it to him?"

"Didn't have it to give."

"I thought he was making his bundle at the steel mill."

"I thought so too. He said something about a wedding ring."

"He's getting married?"

"He says he is."

"Who would marry Harry?"

"He didn't get far enough into it to explain. Once he figured out I wasn't going to cough up he remembered some pressing business that needed doing."

"Right," said Lee.

"Yeah," said Lee's father. He took a drink and cleared his throat. "What about your mother?"

"She's good."

"You talk with her?"

"On the phone, yeah. Sometimes she writes."

"You write her back?"

"Sure."

"Write your mother back, Lee."

"I do."

"She's okay?"

"Seems good, yeah."

"Good but not very good?"

"She seems happy, Dad."

"She get married again?"

"No, no."

"She ask about me?"

"She hasn't."

"She ever tell you why she went off like that?"

"She never explained it to you?"

"Not to my satisfaction."

"You must have some idea, though."

"I know what happened, but not why."

"Okay, what happened?"

"Well, it was mysterious. I mean we weren't Mr. and Mrs. Passionate Obsession, but we never did fight, did we?"

"You didn't, no."

"Which is more than I can say for most. And I'd thought we were on the same page of: this is all right, right here, you know? This'll do. Then one day we're watching a kissing movie on the television and she turns to me with this funny, crooked smile on her face, and she's pointing at the screen and she says, 'I never loved you the way we're promised we'll feel love.' Which, as you can imagine, didn't make me feel great; but I also didn't think it was true, because at the start, she and me—it was a very friendly situation. So I said, 'In the beginning you did. You did feel that way in the beginning.' But she's shaking her head at me, still smiling, and says, 'No, I never did. I never did used to feel the way we were promised we're going to feel.' So, now I'm getting a little mad, right? Because why's she smiling? By which I mean, what is there to smile about at this moment? And why's she bringing this down onto my head after however many years it's been? I'm getting offended on behalf of the work we both put into this thing of ours and I said to her, 'Well, I *did* used to. I *did* used to feel that way.' And I told her that I went into our bargain with a straight heart, right? And that I'd meant it when I recited the vows. What happened later? Our drifting the way we did? That was out of my control and I don't think it was anybody's fault, just what happens in a marriage sometimes, most times. But I was straight, you know, in the beginning. And by now she's stopped smiling, and she says to me, 'Well, I guess I wasn't straight.' And I said, 'I guess you weren't.' And we watched the rest of the kissing movie and went to sleep and all the next day she wouldn't talk or get up out of bed, and day after that she got up but still wasn't talking much other than to make little muttering statements, and the day after *that*, she wakes up, wakes me up, says, 'I'm going to go live with my brother in Billings.' And by God, that's exactly what she did."

The waitress came over, bill in her hand. "Did he eat up his egg?" She set the bill face down on the table. "No rush on that," she said.

"No," said Lee's father, "let's get it settled now, before Internal Revenue storms the restaurant." He passed up a ten-dollar bill, his hand steady. She went off to make change; Lee's father took a drink. He gave a little jolt. "Hold on. Where's your Ford?"

"I sold it."

"Why would you do that?"

"I needed the money."

"Why?"

"I told you I'm going to New Jersey."

"But why? What is the function of your mission? Is

it my imagination or do you not know what in the hell you're doing right now?"

"No, I know," said Lee. He removed the draft notice from his shirt front pocket, unfolded it, and passed it to his father. His father read it and passed it back.

"So, what, you're going to tootle around in that little ballet slipper until the war's over?"

"I guess I'm thinking of leaving."

"Leaving what?"

"Leaving the country."

"And then what?"

"And then not going to Vietnam."

Lee's father said nothing to this but looked away, over Lee's shoulder.

Lee asked, "What do you think about what I just told you, Dad?"

"I don't know. I guess I don't understand what you're talking about."

"You think I should go."

"Of course I do."

"Can I ask why?"

"That's the deal."

"But it's a lousy deal, isn't it?"

"It's a hard thing, sure. But there's something to it, too. Way I look at it, I paid my way in World War Two."

"Paid your way to what?"

"Hold my head up in the United States of America."

Lee didn't know what to say to this; he opted to say nothing. He asked, "Do you remember when they sent you your draft notice?"

Lee's father scowled. "I didn't wait around to be drafted, Leland, you know that. Day after Pearl Harbor I was first in line at the recruitment office. Later I went over and told my folks what I'd done. My mother burst out crying, and the old man kept shaking my hand, proud as hell."

"And didn't it cross your mind that maybe you wouldn't go?"

"I couldn't get over there fast enough. You'd hear about conscientious objectors, but that was fringe stuff—I never set eyes on one. We put the COs in the same folder as the child molesters and religious freaks. The idea of not answering the call was more or less unheard-of. That's your generation's contribution to the culture. Cheers." They clinked coffee cups and Lee drank his coffee and Lee's father drank his coffee and bourbon.

Lee said, "Do me the favor of admitting it's a hard war to get behind."

"Sure, I'll go along with that. But we don't get to pick our wars, Lee."

"No."

"The war they give you, that's your war. And you can drag your heels and bellyache all you want, but you're talking to me about abandoning your own country, and I really don't know what you expect me to say about that other than, buddy, I wouldn't do it if I were you."

"Okay, but don't you think it's weird that they expect us to go over there and murder strangers?"

"You want to get to know them first? Play canasta? Don't forget that the strangers are trying to murder you."

"Don't you think *that's* weird?"

"I think it's unfortunate. But that's just the way it goes, isn't that right?"

"Is it?"

"Yes, it is. That's the way it's always gone and will always go. Cavemen went to war, and so will spacemen. It's just a part of the male American experience. And if you leave your country, that's your business, but as soon as you step over that line, you'll be losing a piece of yourself you won't get back."

This sounded fancifully paranoiac to Lee; but then, if there was nothing to what Lee's father was saying, why his hesitation to leave? It was a wearying topic just then, and Lee was feeling duller all the time, and that he had to sleep. He asked his father if there were still sheets on his bed and his father answered, "Some of the big personality dogs have claimed your bed for their own. Why don't I run you home and you can take my bed and sleep the day away if you want to. If you're still around when I'm off work we can see about dinner somewhere."

Lee's father drove Lee back to the house to drop him off, traveling now at the legal rate of speed. Lee entered the house, pushing through the dogs to shut himself up in his father's bedroom. He lay down on the bed but the bedding reeked, the dogs in the living room were raucous, and his mind was muddled in sorry confusion at the state of his father's life and the reality of what had happened or was happening to his own. When the smell of the sheets became unbearable, Lee stood to open a window and saw that his father hadn't left but was sitting upright in the panel van with his eyes shut and arms crossed, either sleeping or going to sleep. Lee lay back down but the smell overwhelmed him and he stripped the bed, stuffing the sheets in the closet. He fell asleep on the bare mattress; three hours later he was stirred by the muffled ringing of a telephone. Lee followed the sound and located the phone at the bottom of a pile of dirty laundry pushed into the corner of the room. He picked up the phone and said, "Hello," and Grace said, "Lee?"

"Yeah."

"How's Dad?

"Dad's bad."

"Bad how?"

"Bad sad."

"What's all that barking?"

"It's dogs."

"Dogs in the house?"

"There's a houseful of dogs, yeah."

"Why?"

"It's just a whole unique deal Dad's got going on."

"Tell me."

"I'll tell you later."

"Is he there listening or something?"

"No, he's sleeping."

"How's he sleeping with all that barking?"

"Sleeping as in sleeping one off. And he's not in the house, he's out in the van." Lee moved to the window. "Wait, no, the van's gone."

"Sorry, what van are we talking about?"

"Dogcatcher van."

"Dogcatcher van."

"Yeah. I get the sense he's pretty much living out there, actually. He's got a little fixings bar set up in the glove box—aspirin, apple sauce, dental floss, you name it. It's like a miniature store."

"Apple sauce and dental floss in the glove box of the dogcatcher van," said Grace.

"That's right," Lee said. "It's a time, that's for sure. In a nutshell I'd say the old man's gone more or less to pieces."

"He's drinking?"

"Yeah, but it's not that he's drunk so much as, you know, funny-acting."

"Funny-acting how?"

"Making funny-acting decisions? Doing and saying funny-acting things? It's all very depressing in pretty much every way it can be depressing, and now I'm going to change the subject."

"Change it," Grace agreed.

"How are you? Since yesterday? Have you got any updates on your hospital soap opera?"

"As a matter of fact I do, and now I'll give you a hint. I didn't get a lot of sleep last night—and it was not on account of insomnia."

"Oh, boy."

"Yeah."

"You were such a nice girl growing up."

"Was I? I don't know if I was. There's so little in the way of potential for debauchery in Concrete."

"And what does this sleepover mean in terms of where you stand in the larger story?"

"We didn't get around to that topic of discussion."

"Why spoil the mood?"

"That's absolutely right." She let out a long yawn. "What about Mom? You going to go see her, right?"

"I think so."

"What's that mean? You can't see Dad and not Mom."

"I can't?"

"You shouldn't."

"I'll probably go see her."

"You should."

"I will."

"Good boy. Oh, hey, guess what?"

"What?"

"I talked to brother Harry today. Eighteen months with no word and now he calls from beyond the blue."

"Dad says he reached out a little minute ago looking for a loan."

"That's why he called me too, yeah."

"Dad says he says he's getting married."

"No, that's old news. Now he's not."

"What happened?"

"I don't know, because he didn't tell me other than to say it's splitsville."

"How'd he sound?"

"The same, but tireder. I told him you were going to be going by."

"Going right on by, that's right."

"Stop and say hello to Harry, Jesus."

"I don't think I will, thank you. You didn't give him money I hope?"

"A little."

"How much is a little?"

"Wired him fifty bucks."

"You'll never get it back."

"So what?"

"Yeah."

"You know what I mean?"

"I guess. I just think he's—I think our brother's a mutant, Grace."

"Yeah."

"Am I wrong?"

"No, you're not. But the way I see it is that he's got a lot of fear in his heart and that it makes him act unbecomingly. Anyway, Lee, you might be gone a long time, and I think it'd be a handsome gesture for you to stop and say goodbye to your family, each of us."

"God knows I love a handsome gesture."

"Well, you do. And I'm appealing to that particular part of you."

"Okay, but I just genuinely don't *like* Harry, you know?"

"Neither do I, but if I were driving past I'd stop in and refreshen my experience of not liking him and see if there was anything I could do to make him ever so slightly more likable."

"Why?"

"Handsome gesture."

"For the benefit of whom?"

"The handsome gesture exists for itself."

"I'll think about it."

"Okay, but think about it."

"I just said I'd think about it."

"I know, but I'm saying—really do."

Lee said he would, said goodbye, hung up, looked

around the room, feeling sorrowful and emptied out and that it was past time for him to leave. He took a shower, took a white cross, wrote his father an unconvincing note of thanks, and left the house, holding back the dogs as he slipped sideways out the door. He was warming up the Jaguar when he noticed the stooped figure of Mrs. Whitman shuffling across the road to meet him. Her mouth was moving, her right arm held up above her head, hand flapping at the wrist. Lee rolled down his window to receive her.

"There I was," she said, "sitting in my kitchen looking out at the day and who do I see but Lee Clarke, come home from the coast, come for a visit after two long years. Well, I started tidying up in advance of his arrival, put the oven on to heat up last night's pie, and then it happens I'm waiting, waiting—when's he going to knock on the door? And then he never does! And now what, he's driving away in a race car? When I knew him in diapers? When he threw up in my hair at Frontier Days?"

"Hello, Mrs. Whitman, how are you?"

"I'm all right, and thank you very much for asking. How are you?"

"Fine."

"How's California?"

"I like it."

"Sunny?"

"It's sunny a lot of the time."

"Dirty?"

"Parts are dirty, parts are clean."

"I suppose you've visited—your father." Lee nodded and Mrs. Whitman leaned against the car, her voice low, confidential. "You see how it is with him?"

"I do see, yeah."

"You know he won't even speak to me anymore? Drops his eyes each time I say hello? Living in a private world of personal shame? The man needs a good sitting down. The man needs things explained to him."

"Well, he understands he's in the wrong, I think. He's sick, is what it is. He needs to go to a sanitarium."

"What he needs is his family. To help him make arrangements." She squeezed Lee's arm. "It's a good thing you've come. You were always going to be the one, weren't you?"

"The one what?"

"The worthy one."

"I thought Grace was the worthy one."

"No, it was you."

"Well, thank you. But I'm not staying, Mrs. Whitman."

"You're not?"

"I can't."

"Why not?"

"I just can't."

"Have you made arrangements?"

"I haven't."

"Who will make them?"

"I can't say."

She stood up straighter, looking down at Lee with half-shut eyes. "Well then, that's it, I suppose. But I want to go on record saying that I think it's wrong the way you all just ran off and left the man in his hour of need."

"It's been longer than an hour," said Lee.

"Everyone's got his version."

"Sure."

"The story he tells to let himself off the hook."

Lee revved the engine slightly. He had had enough of Mrs. Whitman. She pointed at the sound but looked at Lee. "That's just fine," she said. "But it's a sad day when a child shows his father his back. And now I've said what I wanted to say and you can go on home to California and enjoy your trash and sunshine, Leland Clarke."

Lee watched her walk away and disappear into her home. He could hear the muted barking of the dogs next door and he turned to watch their faces clamoring at the living room window. A feeling came over him, some heady blend of sadness and hate, and he got out of the car and crossed the street and opened the front door. The dogs poured across the threshold in a heave, spilling onto the lawn, into the fresh air, the open space. Some took their liberty at a sprint, vanishing up the road or into the woods, others walked off at an unfussy trot. Some came together to tussle on the grass while some lay down in the sunshine to wag their tails and chew at sticks. A few had remained indoors and Lee made a sweep of the house to usher the stragglers outside, then shut the door and returned to the Jaguar. As he drove away, a half dozen of the wilder dogs gave chase in a pack, barking and howling in his wake. They believed it was their volume and ferocity that forced him down the road, and so were gratified, and one by one began peeling off. By the time Lee got to the highway the dogs were gone and he was thinking of other things.

THE SIEGE OF THE CASCADES AND ROCKY MOUNTAINS

THE HEADY FEELING ENDURED, PROPPED UP AND AMplified by the Benzedrine, and prompted in Lee the wish to engage in dramatic gesture, which begat a plan to best both the Cascades and the Rocky Mountains in one unyielding jump, a siege against nature, a test of mettle, the sightseer's curiosity set aside and in its place the lone consideration of movement, an advancement of the easterly direction. He drove for eight hours and was more or less sober as he pulled into Missoula. It was 10 p.m. and the heady feeling was gone and he felt struck by a soul-tiredness, and that he should like to regroup and rest his eyes from the endless blip of the road's white lines. He pulled into a gas station and filled up the Jaguar and shut himself away in a phone booth. He was lonely, and feeling sorry for himself, and that he missed Cal, and he called her but she didn't pick up. He called his sister but she didn't pick up. He called his mother, who did pick up, and when she did he said, "Mother."

"The Red Hot Topic himself," she answered. "I was wondering when you'd call. Your name has been uttered many times these last few days."

"By who?"

"Whom. Grace and myself, mainly. Afterward and again with your uncle Wallace, who you'll recall expects me to memorize and re-create each conversation I take part in in his absence. Have you sensed your name chewed about in our mouths?"

"I haven't."

"That's disappointing. I wonder if it's that you weren't paying attention? Of course I know that you're—in transit. Possibly you've been distracted by all the dazzling washroom graffiti."

"Possibly," Lee said.

"I heard a man on the television say that graffiti is the hieroglyphic of the modern age. What do you think of that?"

"I think that sounds fine."

"The hieroglyphic of the modern age, and that these

godless scribbles are a mirror held up to our faces. I had a mind to write him a letter and point out that if they hold up a mirror, it's held up to the faces of the men alone. Because women simply don't do that, you know."

"What, never?"

"Never."

"I find that hard to believe."

"You may take my word for it or live in doubt." She paused. "It's late for calls, Leland."

"Sorry, Mom. I thought you'd want an update."

"I did, and do, it's true. And I was up worrying anyway, so I suppose it's no harm done."

"What are you worrying about?"

"About you and about Grace."

"What are you worrying about about Grace?"

"That she is making all the time-honored mistakes of the young female, namely: seeing lust as love, impulse as need, and the fulfillment of desire as noble no matter the mess it makes. The young, male and female alike, always want to think of a life as innately valuable. But it is only valuable if you create a worthy story around yourself."

"Grace is creating a story."

"But not worthy. And neither is yours worthy, by the sound of it and if I may say as much."

"Say away," said Lee.

"Is it true that you're coming to see us?"

"It's true."

"How long will you stay?"

"Not very long."

"One hour?"

"Overnight."

"What size party would you like?"

"I don't want any size party."

"Possibly a small party, or very small?"

"No party, Mom."

"Well how shall we mark the occasion?"

"The occasion will mark the occasion."

"You sound like a crazy fortune cookie."

"I don't feel like one."

This prompted a laugh from Lee's mother, and he basked in the sound, having always wished to please her, and from an early age. "Is there anything you'd like me to bring?" he asked.

"Yourself, most importantly. But also, yes, please do bring an explanation as to why you've made this decision to flee the country of your birth without even mentioning it to your mother. Or would you care to explain it now?"

"Let's wait for the occasion."

"It is correct that you're fleeing?"

"Fleeing isn't the word I'd use."

"Why not?"

"It's the wrong word."

A pause, and Lee knew his mother was reaching for the dictionary, something she often did both on and off the telephone. There came the hushing of shuffled pages, and she cleared her throat. "'*Flee*: To run away, as from danger or evil. To shun or evade. To fly, as a bird or an arrow.'"

"I like the last part."

"But you see my point."

"I do see yours; do you not see mine?"

"What I see is that you want it both ways."

"What ways do you mean?"

"You want to sidestep the skirmish without the judgment of your fellows."

"I want to sidestep the skirmish and what comes from it, comes."

"Possibly you think you're heroic in your turning away."

"The myth of the hero is at the heart of my critique of the entire exercise." Lee thought for a moment. "I didn't expect you to support me in this, but I'm surprised that you'd want me to go over there."

"I didn't say that I want that."

"What do you want?"

"I just don't know yet. That's why I bring it up, to come to an understanding of my own point of view." Lee heard the dictionary clap shut. "What is giving me pause, Leland, is my own biography. Remember that my father's combat record was pure valedictory, and that he came home from the First World War looking just like a film star, as did his two brothers. Not a mark on them, and all three sharp as tacks and quite ready to dance. They were lauded with a parade from one end of town to the other, so smart in their uniforms, sitting shoulder to shoulder in the backseat of a black Cadillac convertible. To my child's mind they had tri-handedly dispatched the Huns and I have never in my life known pride and adoration anywhere near the shrill pitch I knew it in those early days of their return. So it is the photogenic model of my youth working against your contemporary interests, do you see?"

Lee said, "I don't want to be in a parade."

"That's good news, because you're not going to be."

Lee paused. "I was calling to say hello."

"Hello, Lee. Please understand that I could never be truly against you. I just don't want you to do anything to compromise your élan vital."

"God forbid."

"Yes, actually. Forbid it, God, please." She cleared her throat but it came forth as a gentle growl. "Where will you sleep tonight, may I ask?"

"Motel."

"And when will you arrive tomorrow?"

"Afternoon."

"And what do you wish to eat for dinner?"

"Surprise me."

"My son on the run wants a surprise?"

"Yes."

"Fine," said Lee's mother. "Well, I can hardly wait to see you."

"Clearly," said Lee, and his mother told him that sarcasm was uglifying, but that she loved him, perhaps the most of all the children, one wasn't supposed to say it but there it was, the truth laid bare, one might do what one wished with it, if he quoted her she'd deny it to the death, and in parting she asked that Lee should please do her the ultimate favor of traveling with safety at the prow of his mind, and he said that he would, and she hung up the phone, and Lee returned to the Jaguar but didn't start the car, he sat and stared at the world, or one small part of it.

BILLINGS

LEE'S MOTHER APPEARED IN THE DOORWAY OF THE house as Lee came up the steps, and her hair was shorter and grayer, and she wore no makeup but her cheeks were flushed, her eyes shining, and she held herself generally as one in possession of a satisfying secret. She was wearing blue jeans and a pale blue men's button-up shirt. She was removing a pair of gardening gloves. "Leland," she said, leaning in to kiss his cheek. "You're just in time." She led him through a wood-paneled parlor, then a gleaming, white-tiled kitchen, past a screen door, and down a set of creaking steps to the backyard. Running the length of the fence was a tall wall of wildflowers in full bloom. "Can you believe this? They've come into their own all at once, in spite of their variousness." She gripped his arm at the bicep. "Outrageous—outrageous forms and colors!" Lee nodded along but he lacked his mother's enthusiasm; he had taken a white cross with his morning coffee but its effects were dimming, and his mother could see that he was low, and she tugged his earlobe and told him, "You're unwell."

"I'm tired," he said. Stepping away from his mother, he took a turn around the yard, studying the flowers, and the way the honeybees went about their business. The late afternoon sun beat down on his face and felt good and comforting. His mother stood watching him from across the yard. "Won't you say what you think of the house?" she said.

"I think it's very pretty."

"This is where your mother lives."

Lee saw by the tilt of her head and the way she spoke with quiet self-amusement that his mother was happier than she'd been in Concrete; and he was relieved not to be in conflict about this, as he had feared he might be. He looked at his mother looking up at the house, shielding her eyes from the sun.

"It's lucky that we held on to it," she said. "But of course that's all Wallace's doing, as you know."

"I don't know," Lee said.

"Come, sit with me." She waved him over to a bench

beneath a chinaberry tree in the corner of the yard. He crossed the yard and they sat and she spoke and he listened.

She and her older brother Wallace had grown up in the house, purchased by their parents in 1910. Their father had gone to fight in the First World War in 1917, returning the next year in apparent good health but dying by aneurysm only ten years after his homecoming, still a young man at forty-four. Lee's mother was living at home; Uncle Wallace was working as a broker for a real estate firm in New Mexico. They both were present for the funeral, but soon after, Lee's mother accepted a marriage proposal from Lee's father—they had met through a pen pal correspondence organized by the Rotary Club—and moved to Washington state, while Wallace chose to stay behind, to manage over the household and see to their mother, whose health was poor and whose soul was in decline. It was never fully understood what was the matter with Lee's grandmother; hers was a story of both frailty and tenacity—she clung to life, only just barely, but for many years. When she finally died, and the moment arrived that Wallace should return to the world, he found himself reluctant to commit. "After all, there was no pressing need that he should leave, what with the house paid for and his own expenses at the level next to nil. And so what did he do? He paused. Decades passed. We'd kept in touch but I hadn't seen much of him since

Mother's funeral. When I came back here it was plain that he had become, in the interim and in absence of anything like a social life, an eccentric."

"Eccentric how?" Lee asked.

"Disinterest in healthful ways, unreliable hygiene rituals, eating only from tins, keeping objects in the freezer that did not need freezing, establishing a feeding routine with a band of raccoons. Wally needed rehumanizing, and so I rolled up my sleeves. It was good to have work to do in that it distracted me from my troubles, but it was not a joyful period for either of us."

"He was not glad you were here?"

"Not glad, no. He's still not glad. Though of course he is a little glad. And sometimes, once a season, or twice, he's glad in the fuller sense." She sat remembering. "The raccoons were the hardest of his habits to break. I saw that he knew a bond with the animals; and I took this for a sign that there was still some undead ember in there somewhere, and this proved to be the case. He has made a return to the living, is the cheering news; but plain gladness is uncommon here, for our relationship is never simple, for we are not simple people."

"Where is Uncle Wallace now?" asked Lee.

"He's in his room, and likely napping, but it's time he's up anyway." She looked at her watch. "Yes, wake him. I'll meet the pair of you in the kitchen." She stood and looked down at Lee. "Are you happy you've come?"

"I'm happy to see you."

"Are you, though?" She didn't wait for an answer but turned and walked off, leaving Lee alone on the bench in the garden with his thoughts and tiredness. A breeze crossed the yard and the wildflowers bowed and bobbed and the bees were tumbled, their good work devolved to chaos.

Lee returned to the house and tried this and that door in a long hallway with walnut wainscotting and a threadbare runner. He found Uncle Wallace's room; his uncle lay atop his bedspread, gently dozing in slacks and socks, a button-down shirt, and sweater vest. He was pink and plump and unlined and looked, Lee thought, like a baby dressed as a banker. Lee clapped once, loudly, and his uncle's eyes popped open and he asked the ceiling, "What? What is it? What's wrong? What's happened?"

"Hello Uncle Wallace, nothing's happened, it's Lee."

"Oh, Lee. My goodness, you terrified me." He leaned up on an elbow and regarded his nephew. "So you've made it in one piece and in advance of John Law?"

"Made it."

"But you're not home free yet?"

"Not yet."

"And are you feeling waves of great bitterness at the lunatic machinery of mankind pulling you into its grim mechanisms in opposition to your wishes and against the commonsense morals of Mother Nature?"

"Yes."

Uncle Wallace stretched and unstretched. "I find yours a romantic crime. Freedom at all costs and hang the consequences! Your mother is less enamored, but that's to be expected when you consider her unrelenting nature. Well, we've made the decision to play the neutral hosts so much as is possible. Which isn't to say we're not going to talk about it, because we are. But not for very long, and hopefully without any unsightly passion."

"That's fine."

Uncle Wallace sat up, his legs hanging off the side of the bed, feet hovering some inches above the floor. "How long has it been since we've visited? Not since I made my westward quest, I'd say?"

Lee had a memory of his uncle coming to Concrete when he was twelve or thirteen, and that he'd invited himself along to the river, sitting with Lee among his crowd of peers. When he took off his shirt his bosom was ample for a man, so that after, at school, Lee's friends took to asking how his aunt's visit had been. Beyond this, there were friendly cards at Christmas, and once in a while Lee's mother would put them on the phone to say hello. Lee had always had a sense of liking his uncle, without quite knowing who he was, but understanding he lived in a state of apartness, which was not to say unhappiness.

It was dark and close in the room, and Lee could smell talcum powder on the air. Uncle Wallace picked up a pack of cigarettes from his nightstand. He lit one and let out a great bloom of smoke, backlit by the reddish dusky sunshine coming through the split in the curtain. "Where is she?" he asked, and they made for the kitchen, where they found Lee's mother standing in a hunch, peering into the oven. "Surprise, it's meat loaf. And it won't be ready for fifteen more minutes." She shut the oven door and stood, watching her son and brother as they took their seats. "Have you boys been visiting?"

"We've said our hellos, if that's what you're implying," said Uncle Wallace.

"Last you saw Lee he was just a sapling, and now look what's happened."

"A full-grown criminal."

"Pausing his phase of flight to visit with his mother."

"His mother and his uncle."

They both were watching Lee as though his life were a light comedy.

"He looks a little mangled," Uncle Wallace observed.

"Shall I bring him a cup of coffee?"

"Bring the pot," said Uncle Wallace, and Lee's mother did this, poured Lee a cupful, sat opposite him, stared awhile, then commenced her interrogation, first into his own life's details, then Grace's, and finally Harry's. The interrogation was thorough and lasted up to the commencement of the meal. Having plated and distributed the meat loaf, Lee's mother returned to her seat and asked

Uncle Wallace, "What does it mean that each of my three children is in romantic straits? Am I to blame for all?"

"I fear we must say yes."

"Must we?"

"Much of the blame is due you, surely." Uncle Wallace turned to Lee. "They say that the broken home presents the model for the young, who then go forth and re-create that blighted landscape. Are you familiar with the theory?"

"Yes," said Lee.

"But do you have faith in it?"

"Not particularly."

"That's a good boy," said Lee's mother. "And what about the fact that I am not in romantic straits any longer? My days are sane and fruitful and without agony; mightn't my children re-create that?"

"No, the heart mimics only the darker stories," answered Uncle Wallace.

Lee's mother said, "Wallace plucks theories from the clouds, but never with any evidence."

"There's evidence."

"And what is it?"

"The portrait of our society at present."

Lee's mother scoffed. "That's nothing better than cynicism."

"What's wrong with cynicism?"

"It's a dullard's shortcut."

Uncle Wallace said, “Cynicism is a comfort to the user, as it brings a pleasing, meanish joy.” He lifted his fork and took a bite of the meat loaf. “Excellent.”

“Is it?” Lee’s mother also took an interested bite. “Yes, it’s very nice.”

Lee was looking at his meat loaf but hadn’t eaten any and didn’t want to, as his stomach was agonized. But he took a bite to appease his mother, who sat by awaiting his opinion. “It’s good,” he said.

“Is it good? Well, that’s better than bad, certainly.”

“It’s great, Mom. I’m sorry.” He set his fork down. “I’m lousy company right now. I’ve been taking pep pills to make time.”

“Well, they aren’t working, because you’re not peppy at all.”

“I’ve taken too many.”

“Not enough, it seems. Would you like another coffee?”

“Yes.”

Lee’s mother refilled Lee’s coffee cup. She offered her brother more and he covered his cup with his hand. She poured herself a cup and told Lee, “Grace tells me you saw your father, and that he is now a dogcatcher?”

“Right.”

“Personally he catches them?”

“Yes.”

“With a net?”

"He wags meat at them."

"What?"

"He says he wags meat at them."

Lee's mother looked to her brother. "Perhaps the situation is not so bad as it sounds."

"No, it is," said Lee.

"The man is not thriving?"

"Not thriving."

"And how does this make you feel about your mother?"

"I love my mother."

"But is she not an abandoner?"

"I guess she is. That doesn't make her a villain, though, does it?"

"Does it?"

"I don't see that it has to." Still, and his mother looked disappointed; Lee asked her, "Would you like a scolding?"

"I think I would, actually. But only if you felt the need."

"I don't."

"Fine, but if you did, if you do, then you must speak up now. For none of us can say when the opportunity will come again."

"I don't feel the need."

"Is it not healthful to speak of hard things?" she asked Uncle Wallace, who was looking into space and didn't appear to be listening.

"But I don't have anything to say about it," said Lee.

"And what if I do?"

"Then you should go ahead."

"Because I want you to understand me."

"It's fine, go on."

"You're sure?" she asked, and he nodded, and she assumed the storyteller's proud posture. "Just that my leaving was not in response to a sudden impulse, or whim," she said. "I had hidden away my heart's condition for years, but then came the threshold where I could no longer pretend I wasn't unhappy, because the pretending was making me ill." She was silent a moment. "The problem had to do with your father."

"Right."

"What I'm saying is, my decision to leave was not related to you and your sister and brother."

"Yes, we understood that."

"You three weren't surprised when I ran off?"

"No, we were. Because there didn't seem to be anything the matter with the two of you that wasn't the matter with everyone else's parents. But we knew when it happened that we weren't to blame." Lee paused. "I noticed you'd been quiet the last few months before you left."

Uncle Wallace shivered and spoke: "Living in a crouch."

"That's exactly right," said Lee's mother. "I was working myself into a sort of trance ahead of my leave-taking.

Conditioning myself for the moment I should make my confession and bolt."

"Like a thief in the night in the day," Uncle Wallace said.

Lee's mother wagged a finger at her brother. "I knew and still know a guilt at the fact of my going away, but it was not the guilt of the thief, because I was not stealing anything, but taking back that which had been stolen from me."

"Gee," said Uncle Wallace.

Lee said, "Dad says you were watching a movie."

"What?" Lee's mother asked sharply.

"He says you were watching a movie, and that's what brought it all up."

"Did he, now?" She sat back. "And what else did he say?"

"Not so much."

"But you must have sensed a summarizing tone."

Lee said, "Confusion tone."

"Confusion in what way?"

"In the way of not understanding what happened."

"My motivations, you mean? I was so plain about that, though; and I went to the trouble of stating the hard words." Lee's mother thought. "Do you feel the confusion is genuine? Or do you think he's telling you a story?"

"The confusion is genuine," said Lee.

She shook her head. "I find that remarkable, insulting, and depressing."

"What about the movie?" asked Uncle Wallace.

"What about it?"

"Was there one or wasn't there?"

"There was, but he's wrong if he thinks that was the one moment, because there wasn't one moment, but hundreds of moments, many hundreds. The horror of the dull marriage is not just that nothing is happening, but that the other person is so frequently there *doing* the nothing, so that you not only live beside the nothingness, but watch its realization each day. That man would sit in his lounge chair for phases of an hour, two hours, and it was as if the extent of his function was to maintain a state of living, the inhalation and exhalation of oxygen, feeding the brain and heart."

Uncle Wallace said, "Perhaps he'd achieved enlightenment, like the yogis in the Far East who sit on beds of nails and are said to occasionally levitate."

"Yes, well, if he'd levitated, I might have stayed."

"Right." Uncle Wallace looked away, then back. "May I ask a hard question, but fair?"

"You may."

"Why would you marry a man that should make you feel this way?"

"Naturally it was a different kettle of fish at the start,

Wallace. Particularly when we were writing letters to and fro, I found him so droll, and there was a musical aspect to his prose that made me see him as artistic in temperament. Certainly there was a sense of potential. It was not overpowering, but I was young and more familiar with the optimist's outlook. Then the children came along, and that was my glad activity for however many years; but by the time they reached adolescence, they were more or less independent, and so there was less to distract me. There stood my husband, the first good look I'd had in some time, and he had become his father, stooped and humorless, and the content of our conversations made me feel that I'd flunked the big test." She took a bite of the meat loaf. "I suspected my situation was not going to improve. Time passed and I knew that the suspicion was correct, and soon after came the threshold. In a fit of factual, that is to say true desperation, I decided I'd done the job, and the job was done, and I would go, and that was all there was to it. I sent a telegram to Wallace that I was coming for a visit, and to ready my room. The next day I was away."

"The telegram did not say 'coming for a visit,'" Uncle Wallace told Lee. "It said 'coming for a visit to stay.' I'd thought it a badly formed sentence, but when I saw her eyes, I understood."

"It had been a long trip. Longer than the time it took to get here, if you know what I mean."

"Yes, but tell the story of it."

"You know the story of it."

"Tell it for Lee."

"Lee doesn't want to hear it."

"I'd hear it," said Lee.

"See?" Uncle Wallace pointed at Lee while talking to Lee's mother. "Go on, tell it, dinner and a show. How'd it start?"

Lee's mother said, "It started in the morning, in a state of nervous exhaustion. I called a taxi and pulled out my secretly packed suitcases from under the bed. The taxi was honking and I left the house without saying goodbye. The cabbie was gray, ulcerous, and unkind. He could see that I was in the midst of some distressful situation, and all the way to the bus station he tried to get me to discuss it, but I was in a daze, my answers vague things, murmurs. The cabbie became frustrated; he said, 'I can't help you if you don't tell me what's wrong.' I laughed, and he was offended, and he asked me what was funny about friendliness and I said I didn't know what, but something. He refused my tip and as a parting salvo told me, 'I'd wish you luck, lady, but to tell you the truth you don't look like the type that believes in it.'"

"Rude," said Uncle Wallace.

"It was, and it was meant to be. He wanted to needle me and he succeeded. Because I was fixated on the idea of luck in those days, and had long felt if I could just lay my hands on some of the stuff I'd be in business. But it eluded me and so I feared I had no talent for it."

"For luck," said Lee.

"Luckiness, yes," his mother said. "Next was the bus depot, where I was to spend six hours sitting on a hard bench thinking of what I was actually doing, what it meant about my character, what my leaving might lead to, and etcetera."

"Six hours is a long time," said Uncle Wallace.

"A long time to sit on a hard bench, yes, and with nothing much to do but watch all the comings and goings, the snapshot moments of the lives of the strangers all around me, and each of them was so lost in their particular story, so deeply mired in the performance of it. In studying these people I began to ponder, for the first time in my life, the notion, the role of destiny."

"Destiny," said Uncle Wallace.

"Destiny," said Lee's mother. "Do you know the definition?"

"Yes."

"What is it?"

"I know what the word means. Let us have no dictionaries at the dinner table, please."

"I don't need to look at the dictionary, because I was traveling with my pocket *Merriam-Webster* at the time, and I looked up the word and memorized it and it is: 'the culminating condition, foreordained by the divine will, or by human will, and conceived as a resistless power.' How do you like that?"

"Very nice," said Uncle Wallace.

"The phrase *resistless power* was cheering in that it seemed to absolve me, to imply that I was merely dancing to time's tune, as one had to do. I felt that I was encouraged by my destiny, then; or the force behind my destiny. Not led by it, but advised from the side, a voice saying which way I ought to go." She paused. "Am I making sense?"

"Somewhat."

"I got on the Trailways en route to Billings. Nothing happened, no one spoke, the faces were corpsey, and the Cascades made me lonesome to look at them. There was a two-hour layover in Coeur D'Alene and I took in the downtown area. They were having a sort of jamboree, but it was the third of three days and the crowd was testy and haggard. I saw a balloon vendor arguing with a policeman on a street corner, and the policeman popped one of the vendor's balloons with the ash end of a cigar and the vendor went white in the face with silent rage. I saw a chubby child picking confetti from his mother's hair and eating it. The town was in a sorry state, the trash cans spilling over. Triangulated streamers had been strung up from one end of the main street to the other but it had rained in the night and the streamers had come away and were pasted on the pavement like papier-mâché. Their colors: red, orange, and purple."

"I envy your memory for detail," Uncle Wallace said.

"Perhaps I'm making it all up."

"Are you?"

"I don't think so. But who could ever trust a recollection?" She paused. "A man propositioned me in the diner attached to the bus station. He was very frank about it, and while it wasn't particularly upsetting, it was a bit of a sneaky surprise."

Lee was making an anxious face; his mother patted his arm and told him, "Don't worry, the story doesn't go the man's way."

"What did he say?" asked Uncle Wallace.

"He said, 'I have an apartment nearby, very clean, and discreet.' I told him, 'Oh, isn't that nice?' Because I didn't quite know what he was talking about at first. This apartment announcement was from out of the blue, and was related to nothing that we had been discussing, which up to that point had been our given Christian names. I simply thought him a bird proud of his nest, but then he clarified his wishes when he said, 'How much time do you have? Because I don't like to rush when it comes to lovemaking.'"

"A technician," said Uncle Wallace.

"Confident he could do the work, certainly."

"And what happened next?"

"I paid my bill and wished the man all the luck in the world."

"How did he take the rejection?"

"In stride. I boarded the bus for Billings and settled into my seat. At this stage of the journey I was feeling low, that the world was unwelcoming, and that men could see that I had no protector. I sat there with my troubles held up tight in my fist, wanly marking the characters climbing aboard the idling bus. The last on was a blind woman and her dog, a great drooling brute with bloodshot eyes and a face made up of damp, hanging folds."

"A bloodhound?" Uncle Wallace asked.

"No."

"Basset hound?"

"No."

"Mastiff?"

"I don't know. Be silent. The dog had been trained to lead this woman about, and I watched the clever animal seek out the only empty seat on the bus. The woman sat at the window, the dog beside her on the aisle, facing forward and thinking its doggish thoughts. It was a hot day, and the woman unfolded a fan, and she would fan herself ten or fifteen strokes, then the dog. And when she fanned the dog, it turned its drooling face to meet the breeze, and delicately shut its eyes." Lee's mother shut her eyes, and opened them. "A little charm goes a long way when one is feeling desolate, and I took this small scene as a fortifying clue that the world was not a thorough cesspool. The sun sank, and I slept through the night and dreamed of easy things. In the morning the woman and dog were gone and the bus was on the far side of the Rockies and the air was different, the light was different, and I felt—different."

"Better," said Uncle Wallace.

"Yes. I was still in a state of agitation but there was another reality bubbling up, a sense of accomplishment and pride, and this was sustained. I took a taxi from the bus station and the driver did not harass me, did not see me as one whom he could safely harass, and he took his gratuity with humility."

"He helped with your bags."

"And went promptly and silently away, that's right. And I stood in the front room of my childhood home thinking the thoughts one might expect in such a situation as mine."

"Your condition had culminated."

"That's it. And now you have heard the story of my flight from Washington state to Billings, Montana." A silence passed over the table. Uncle Wallace was watching his sister with a look of secret amusement. "What," she said.

"When are we going to discuss the connection between your stepping away from your family and Lee leaving the country?"

"We can do that now if you like, but I feel there is nothing much to discuss, as your thought is a void."

"You don't see that there is some sameness at play?"

"Apples and oranges."

"Apples and pears."

"Name the sameness."

"Each of you has his boundary, his limit, isn't that so? No matter one's devotion to spouse or country, there is still the untouchable piece of oneself that must not be encroached upon. You each were pressed to accept that which you could not accept, and you did not accept it." He looked at Lee. "Sameness named."

Lee's mother sat considering her brother's words. "I'll admit there is some discomfort caused by the naming of the theory. Can it be that I'm hiding the truth of it from myself?"

"Would that be so outlandish a thing?" asked Uncle Wallace.

"One ought to know how one feels about a given topic, shouldn't one?"

"I should think we all keep quite a lot hidden away from ourselves, all through the day and into the long nights."

"Let's not get carried away." Lee's mother sipped her

coffee, and her face went soft and tranquil. "I was explaining to Lee that Dad's homecoming is informing my opinion of his abstention from war."

"What about Dad's homecoming?"

"Just, the glamor and wattage of him and his brothers. The way the town received them as princes. The parade, the pomp." Lee's mother was smiling within the memory of this; when Uncle Wallace softly snorted, she asked, "Something is amusing?"

"Darkly amusing."

"What is dark?"

"That you continue to recall Dad the way you do." Uncle Wallace told Lee, "I've heard it told so many times by your mother, that our father returned from the war a film star, that he was the golden conqueror, and every citizen wept at the sight of his ribbons and gleaming medals."

"And you take issue with this?" asked Lee's mother.

"I do, because none of it's true, or very little of it."

"Explain yourself."

"Shall I start with the parade?"

"Fine."

"Dad was not a film star at all. He was sodden drunk, propped up by his brothers, who also were drunk. They reeked of rye and each was filled with contempt that they were made to perform for the benefit of those who did not have to go through what they went through, and you are either willfully misremembering the event or, and more likely, you weren't old enough to understand the truth."

"I was old enough."

"Six years old."

"Seven years old."

"Seven years old."

"Perhaps there is your truth and my truth," Lee's mother said.

"Yes, and there must be. But the truth of truths, small sister, is that our father came home from Europe a different man than the one who set out. He was changed, totally, permanently, and not in any way for the better."

Lee's mother's face had taken on a dour affect. She said, "I can accept that I may have added some sparkle to Dad's parade. I *was* a child and there *were* trumpets blowing in my ear and the confetti *was* twirling through dazzling sunshine. But you can't deny the brass tacks of my relationship with him. I knew our father just as well as you did, and not just as a child but a young woman."

"You knew what he showed you; and he didn't show you everything."

"What exactly are you driving at?"

Uncle Wallace asked, "Do you truly not recall the beatings he gave me?"

"Recall the beatings he gave you," said Lee's mother flatly. "No, I don't, actually. I know that you were often in trouble."

"Serious trouble, yes."

"You were bad; he was stern."

"Wrong. Untrue. Incorrect. Our father beat me ragged. Not once but serially, and not for any reason relating to my behavior."

"Well you must have done something, Wallace. Because he never beat me."

"Nor me, until he came home from Europe. Before the war he'd been what I thought of as a regular father, and we did regular father-son things. He was not the warmest man on earth but from time to time he'd wink at me, pat my shoulder. After the war he showed me not the slightest kindness, and once or twice a month he'd come into my room with a demon in his eyes, drag me out to the backyard, and whip me. And when he whipped me, he hated me. I was a proxy for some other thing, but my function in his life was that of a release valve. He was calmer after the beatings, and would give me little presents, or press a dollar into my hand, but then it would start building again, in agonizing degrees, almost at once." Uncle Wallace paused. "I despised our father. He terrified me from the time he came home from the war until I left for New Mexico. And when he died, I felt only relief, only a restfulness."

Lee had been studying his uncle all through the speech, fixated by the calm with which the information was relayed. When his uncle fell silent Lee turned to his mother and saw that her face had gone pale, and she looked stricken as she asked, "Why do you say all this now?"

"I should have said it years ago."

"But why would you speak of such uglinesses when Lee is here?"

"I say it so you know the truth, foremostly; but yes, I also say it as it is relevant to Lee's own current situation."

"In what way is it relevant?"

"That's something you can work out yourself, and without too much trouble, I should think."

Lee's mother sat back, marking her brother as she plotted out her route of counterattack. She was on the cusp of presentation when Lee saw something topple in his mother, a look of hurt surprise came over her face, and she stood and left the room. A long moment passed; Uncle Wallace made small adjustments to the placement of his cutlery. "I've been wanting to burst that bubble for such a long time, but now that I've done it I feel simply caddish. Do you think I should have let her fantasy alone?"

"I don't know what anyone should do about anything," said Lee. He was very deeply tired. Looking at the door his mother had left by, he asked, "Do you think she'll come back?"

"Oh yes, she always returns for dessert." Uncle Wallace pointed at Lee's full dinner plate and Lee shook his head and Uncle Wallace took the plate away and set it in the sink, returning with a raspberry pie, which he placed on a trivet and set to dividing with a long knife. Lee didn't want dessert, and didn't touch his; Uncle Wallace ate with an enthusiasm that was vaguely sickening for Lee to witness. There came a creak of the door; Lee's mother's face appeared. She looked to have been crying, and Uncle Wallace said, "Peek a boo-hoo-hoo." She acknowledged the quip's value with a nod, reentered the room and sat, refolding her napkin across her lap. "You may serve me my dessert in lieu of an apology," she said, and Uncle Wallace did this, solemnly, but with a trace of deviltry at the edge of his eyes and mouth.

This was the last moment Lee could recall before he fell asleep sitting up at the table. He woke at three o'clock in the morning; the room was dark but for the light of the moon, and he was wrapped in a throw blanket. There was a note on the table: *We are too old to move you. You are rude when we try to wake you. In childhood you were a light sleeper.* Lee sought out the guest room and lay atop the bedspread looking at the black square of the ceiling, tireder in this moment than he had ever been in his life, his limbs shooting out in uncontrollable little fits of twitching, tears drawing down the sides of his face and dampening his pillow. He was not crying, but leaking, or oozing. He dropped again into sleep, awakened at dusk, fifteen hours later, by the shrill, twinned screaming of two female children playing in the street; the screaming reverberated within Lee's heart so that he came to in a state of panicked confusion. He showered and shaved and took a white cross. When he entered the kitchen, suitcase in hand, he found his uncle and mother sitting at the table, and Lee's mother was looking up a word in the dictionary, with Uncle Wallace staring victimishly into space. Lee's mother cleared her throat. "'*Transmute*: to change from one nature, form, or substance into another; to transform; as to *transmute* mercury into gold, one species into another, or sorrow into joy.'" She closed the dictionary. "One must know what one means before one speaks; and when he speaks he must state the idea in its fullness, and with accuracy." Uncle Wallace turned to Lee. "Murder me quickly, and without suffering."

Lee's mother was looking coldly at Lee's suitcase. "What is this, you're leaving?"

"Yes."

"Now?"

"Yes."

"Don't you want anything to eat?"

"No thank you."

"Fine." She sighed and stood. "I will walk you out. Say goodbye to your nephew, Wallace." Uncle Wallace stood to face Lee, taking up his hand to shake it. "Good luck, Lee," he said. "Sorry about all the bastards." Lee thanked his uncle and followed his mother through the parlor and to the front porch. She leaned against the face of the house, at a remove and wrapped up in her own arms. "I'm worried there is something between us, now," she said.

"I don't say there is."

"But I can feel the something."

"What would you like me to do about it?"

"I don't know. I don't suppose there is much. But don't think badly of your mother, all right?"

"I've already told you I don't."

"But don't you?"

"No." Lee paused. "Maybe it's that you think badly of yourself."

"Not in the least. I have never wished to hurt a soul, but life sometimes forces the hard hand, and so you must administer the medicine."

"Yes, well, I agree," said Lee; for of course, and just as Uncle Wallace had said, he also saw a connection between his and his mother's stories. Lee's mother understood his thinking and she regarded him with critical suspicion.

"You do not administer the medicine."

"I am taking my medicine."

"You are *not* taking your medicine."

Lee pointed. "It's you who thinks badly of me."

She shook her head. "The world of my youth made flawless sense to me, the songs we sang were joyful and sane. But now the spirit of the time is unrecognizable, and a shroud is descending from the sky. It portends a grim new day, with each person looking out for himself, and the songs the children sing are deranged."

"But you *are* thinking of me badly."

"I am wrestling with the question of my feelings. When I arrive at the place of knowing, then I shall tell you."

"All right."

She came closer, and her eyes were searching. "How will I know that you're safe?"

"I'll call you and tell you."

"But will you?"

"Yes."

"And if you're not safe?"

"Then you'll know it in the marrow of your bones." He smiled as he said it, but the sentiment frightened his mother. She told him he mustn't speak like that, that it was tempting fate, and after all what was a curse but a short line of words strung together? She asked him to take it back, and he did. He stowed his suitcase and sat warming up the Jaguar. His mother was watching sternly from the porch until Wallace called her away, and she turned and disappeared back into the house. Lee put the Jaguar into gear and drove away as quietly as was possible.

THE ANTIPATHY BETWEEN LEE AND HARRY

THE ANTIPATHY BETWEEN LEE AND HARRY HAD BEEN IN evidence from the onset of Harry's adolescence, but to understand Lee's deeper dislike of his brother one had to discuss Marinka Kabulka. At the start of the spring semester of the eleventh grade, Marinka was led into Lee's classroom by the principal. She was a tall, gaunt girl in a drab cotton dress with bagged socks and unshiny buckling shoes. She faced the class with what read as something past boredom, and her gaze was not the gaze of a sixteen-year-old. "This is Marinka," said the principal. "She's come all the way from Budapest. Which is in the country of Hungary. Which is situated in Central Europe. Now, she's had a rough time of it over there, and she's a long way from her people, but she's safe and sound with us in Concrete, and I know you'll do what you can to make her feel welcome, all right? Isn't that right?" A murmuring of unenthusiastic assent from the students; now Marinka stepped forward to address them. Her English was fair but accented, and she spoke in a monotone, staring at the wall at the rear of the room: "Thank you. I am pleased to be here with you. I offer my bond of friendship. Have a nice day, goodbye." No matter the principal's exhortation, Marinka's fellow students did not make her feel welcome. Her eerily placid demeanor caused a disturbance among the student body, the boys fascinated but fearful, the girls fearful, hostile. The alphas, led by Mary McKane, came together to protest Marinka Kabulka, mocking her when she wasn't around, with attentions paid to her plain, perhaps homemade clothing, that she didn't know who the Everly Brothers were, and that she brought her lunch to school wrapped in a faded pink cotton cloth. They whispered that she was lice-ridden, that she washed only weekly, and in the halls the girls discreetly held their noses as they stepped out of her path. Marinka had no reaction to any of it, her face a mask of nonfeeling, something the girls also commented on—was it that she was too ignorant to care what the world thought of her?

She sat in front of Lee at homeroom and first period, and he spent every weekday morning staring at the back of her head: the tight bun pulled up and kept in place with a piece of skinny ribbon, a different color each day, her lone festive or feminine gesture, hardly noticeable, but for Lee a significant detail. She sat alone at lunchtime, under a tree at the far edge of campus, her lunch lain atop the pink cloth. After she ate—the girls commented on the fact that she always ate her lunch to the last crumb, which was true, she did—she snapped the cloth, folded it into a tight square, and tucked it away into the pocket of her dress.

One afternoon in the office Lee overheard the school secretary telling a teacher that Marinka had lost both parents to Communist death squads, and that she'd been relocated to Concrete to live with distant relatives she'd never met before, aged immigrants, backward people who lived in something close to squalor in the woods beyond the river. The next morning, riding his bicycle to school, Lee saw Marinka emerge from the woods to walk along the highway. Her pink cloth, heavy with the lunchtime meal, swung in a lazy pendulum at her side and as Lee passed her by he felt variously adoration, empathy, and desire.

The spring semester passed with Lee watching the back of Marinka's head—the lacquered bun, the ever-changing ribbon—but they never once spoke. In the halls her eyes were turned inward, and he was left to wonder what words moved through her mind. He romanticized her foreignness and suffering and believed her thoughts were made from timeless and wise truths of the soil. One day after school he came upon Marinka and a stooped crone-like woman, presumably her guardian, standing together at the edge of campus, speaking in rapid-fire Hungarian. Marinka's guardian spoke at full volume, and combatively, but Marinka's voice was a low and breathy whisper. There was something in Marinka's shyness at speaking her native language that summoned in Lee a dreamy feeling, and he paused nearby, dropping to a knee to untie and retie his right shoe that he might eavesdrop. The language was unfathomable to Lee, innately virtuosic, like a complicated run of music. He had retied his right shoe twice and now was retying his left when the conversation ceased, and Lee looked up to find Marinka watching him with an expression that explained she knew what he was doing, and that she wished him to stop. Heedful, exhilarated, he stood and walked off, left shoelace unfurled, flapping with each step.

Lee never described his fascination to anyone and believed he was effectively hiding it away but then Mary McKane stopped him outside the locker room after gym class and passed him a note: *Do you love her y/n/m?* Through her own ceaseless study of Marinka Kabulka, Mary McKane had tracked the fact of Lee's frequent nearness, and the wracked look in his eye. He passed the note back, pretending not to understand the question at all, and afterward he was more discreet with his attentions, but Mary must have spread the news around because a few nights later, as Lee's family was settling into their seats at the kitchen table, Harry announced, "Hang your heads in shame, gang. Lee's in love with a Commie." Lee stood and left the room, left the house, the evening air cool across his hot face. He walked to the diner and ate his dinner alone, and he felt very dramatic, and that his life described complex dimensions.

On the last day of school, after the bell had rung and the students were rising from their desks, Marinka shook hands with each of her four neighbors: left hand, forehand, right hand, Lee. If she'd heard the rumors of his affinity for her she gave no indication of it; she looked him in the eye and bowed her head, a simple gesture of goodwill, and Lee carried away with him a sense of admiration for Marinka Kabulka.

Summer break was underway and Lee entered each still, hot day with the hope he might see her somewhere in town, but weeks passed with no sign of her. He didn't delude himself with the idea that she was thinking of him; but he had decided that whenever they finally crossed paths he would engage her, presenting her with his especially authored question: Are you enjoying your summer vacation, Marinka?

Lee and his brother had by this time come into their antipathy in earnest. Harry, nineteen, had sprouted and become brutishly handsome, which when paired with his already abrasively confident personality and his newly acquired Honda Scrambler made him suddenly formidable. He cultivated or was beset by a newer cruelty, which made Lee fear him, and wish to avoid him, and he did avoid him, so much as one can avoid a person he lives with.

The youth of Concrete gathered daily on a shifting strip of sand on the banks of the Skagit River. Lee and Harry were often there at the same time but rarely spoke, and they never once sat together. At the midpoint of the summer, Marinka Kabulka showed up, walking down the little path leading from the highway and toward the water, her same solemn self, only now she wore sunglasses, and her hair was down, and when she removed her cotton dress there was a bathing suit underneath, a red one-piece. She picked a spot among her peers as if it were the usual thing, oiling her long legs and causing a thorough psychic disturbance. Harry walked over to where Lee was sitting. "Who in the hell is that?" he asked, pointing with his chin.

"That's Marinka."

"The Commie?"

"She's Hungarian."

Harry did not hesitate, but walked over to Marinka

and stood above her prone body, blocking her sunlight and addressing her directly. She propped herself on her elbows to look up at Harry, her expression betraying nothing, so that Lee was hopeful she would rebuff him. But when he offered his hand in greeting, she reached up and took it; and then, a moment later, in response to some quip or comment of Harry's, she smiled. In all his moments of studying Marinka Kabulka, Lee had never seen her smile once, not even slightly; he felt a drilling heat in his chest, and he wished to fly away. Now Marinka nodded and stood, collecting her towel and sandals and stepping into her dress. She and Harry walked together up the path and to the highway, speaking easily back and forth, unaware they were being watched by every person on the riverbank.

Harry kicked over the Honda while Marinka dusted the sand from the bottoms of her feet and slipped into her sandals. She climbed onto the back of the bike and gripped Harry at the waist. He called to her over his shoulder and she held him tighter, and now they shot away. After the sound of the Honda's engine could no longer be heard, then did the crowd of teens fall into enthusiastic discussions of what had happened, and what it meant. Mary McKane was thrilled; she hurried over to ask Lee what he made of it and he answered automatically that it was none of his business. He could hear his voice, but it was as if it were coming from another body.

He waited as long as he could, affecting a casual air, but soon he left the beach, pushing his bike up the path and pedaling slowly home to sit in his room beside his nauseous heartsickness.

There followed an evilly long month where Marinka and Harry were often seen in one another's company: at the hot dog stand, or the bowling alley, racing through town on the Honda, making for some meadow or hunter's shack. Lee's unhappiness was profound, and all through this era the two brothers ate dinner together nightly. Harry studied Lee at the table, not with any relish but a blankness, a nonemotion, which somehow was more disturbing than if he'd gloated. Lee thought of his brother in extreme physical pain. He did not want to cause it, but he did wish to witness it.

The story played out to its tragic ending. Marinka's guardians received an anonymous letter describing a torrid public display on the back of a known hooligan's motorcycle, and while Mary McKane never claimed responsibility for the letter, neither did she deny it with any meaningful vigor. Lee was home alone one afternoon when there came a knock on the door, and there was Marinka, a confused expression on her face. "Mr. Shoelaces. What are you doing here?"

"I live here."

"Where is Harry?"

"Out."

"Where?"

"I don't know."

She passed up an envelope. "Give this to him, please," she said. "Don't read it."

"Okay."

She turned and walked off and Lee opened the envelope to find a brief note stating that Marinka was being made to leave Concrete, naming a forwarding address in Maryland. Lee felt relief at the absence of sentimental language; it could almost have been an admonishment. But then he turned the page over to find a finely detailed pencil drawing of a clutch of wildflowers floating in the center of the page, and he understood two things at once: that Marinka was the person he'd thought and hoped she was, and that the letter was a statement or announcement of love. He did not give the letter to his brother but slipped it through the sewer grate out front of his house. He didn't feel that he'd been wrong in doing this, not at the time and not after.

There was no news of Marinka Kabulka forthcoming and it was not so long before Lee left town, and his new life in California blotted out the thought of her. But there was a memory of the injury built into the idea of Harry which summoned, believably if briefly, the old sting of it. And so, heading east in the Jaguar, Lee did not actually want to see Harry very much at all, and he was not in a state of conflict about it. What spurred him on ultimately, what led to his veering upstate and to Duluth was not a sense of familial duty, but a curiosity about what his brother had become. He had an inkling all was not well with Harry, and he wished to see evidence of this, to take his impressions and bring the details back to Grace, that they might swoon over the cold facts of a life badly lived, and wonder at the pure bloodiness of it all.

Lee hit Duluth at nine o'clock in the morning. He parked in front of his brother's home, a modest but tidily maintained bungalow, on a block of modest bungalows. Trudging up the steps, he knocked; his brother's silhouette appeared behind the screen door. "Oh, right," Harry said, then walked away. Lee entered the house to find him slumped on a sofa in a not-bright room, a cigarette in his hand, tucked up high at the knuckle. He was in a bad way, as Lee had believed; his fiancée had left him some days prior and he didn't know what to do about it. Lee sat across from his brother and asked what had happened.

"Caught with my hands in the pickle jar," said Harry.

"Both hands?"

Harry nodded. He made a circling gesture. "It happened here, in this room. I was sitting where I'm sitting now." Harry pointed at a phone on a stand by the entryway. "It rang, she answered it, nodded, hung up, unplugged the phone, carried it across the room, threw it at my head." There was a faded bluish bruising on Harry's forehead below the hairline. He said that the bell inside the phone had dinged when it connected with his skull, and he thought he must have briefly fainted because his next memory was his fiancée leaving with her suitcase, the fireproof lockbox, and car keys.

"Her car or your car?"

"Our car."

"What's in the fireproof lockbox?"

"Assorted important shit, among other things."

Harry stared into space, his state degraded to the point of redoubtability. Lee felt he needed to acclimate before he might face it and stepped away, making a tour of Harry's home, surprised to find it efficiently outfitted: framed prints on the walls, beds made, clean towels in the bathroom. Harry, historically, was not an aesthetic person, and Lee attributed the furnishings to the fiancée. He called from down the hall, "What's the fiancée's name?"

"Sally."

"How'd you meet?"

"I went up to her and said, 'Hi, I'm Harry.'"

"How long has she been gone?"

"Six days. I took the week off work thinking that'd fix me up but I still feel just as horrible as ever." Lee returned to the living room and sat. Harry said, "Now I'm going to describe my emotions to you." He was suffering the suffering of the individual who'd been spotlit in the act of wrongdoing; but also there was another suffering, a second suffering, this stemming from a disappointment in his fellow man. There were some among Harry's social group, he told Lee, who had known he'd been stepping out on Sally, but had for months been keeping this fact from her. Whether this was due to their not wishing to wound her or out of deference to Harry, who could say; the important thing was that a precedent had been set. And so he was shocked that these individuals had suddenly and without warning gone against what he had come to think of as their unspoken contract. Lee listened to this and was familiarly impressed by the depth and richness of his brother's misanthropy. "You're disappointed in these people," he said.

"Well, I am, yes," Harry answered earnestly. "They hurt Sally very badly."

"You did."

"Semantics."

"It's not."

"Let's say we all hurt her."

"It was you."

"Semantics."

"You don't know the meaning of the word, do you?"

"Semantics."

Lee noticed a bandage over Harry's right forearm and asked, "What's that?" Harry looked at the bandage awhile, then worked to peel it back. It was a fresh tattoo, a Vaseline-smeared portrait of a flower-wrapped heart, with a banner unfurling above and below. On the top banner, in emphatic capital letters, were the words

HARRY LOVES

The bottom banner was empty. "It was arranged so that Sally'd come in just when her name was being written out," Harry explained. "But she got there early, which I guess I should be happy for now. She stepped up and saw what I was doing and laughed her head more or less off her shoulders. Walked out of the tattoo parlor just, you know, braying. Me and the tattoo man watched her go, then looked at each other, and he said, 'Finish, not finish?' 'Not finish, I think,' I said. So, it's blank for now."

Lee told Harry, "You could write, 'Long walks on the beach.'"

"Hilarious."

"'His alone time.'"

"Stop." Harry covered the tattoo back up. "It's not a joke, Lee. I've fucked up a good thing. I have fucked *up*. Do you hear what I'm saying? I've fucked up in a whole new way, and I'm very fucked up about it, okay?"

"Okay."

Harry stubbed out his cigarette. He looked at his brother directly for the first time. "You look like shit."

"I've been driving all night. *You* look like shit."

"I *feel* like shit," Harry said reasonably. The phone

rang and he flinched and stared bitterly at it. When it ceased ringing, he turned back to Lee. "What are you up to, anyway? Where are you going?"

Lee pulled out the draft notice and held it out for Harry, who said, "I don't want to read your mail."

"I don't want to read yours."

"Just tell me what it is."

"I've been drafted."

Harry took the envelope, unfolded the letter, and read it. "You're not thinking about dodging?"

"I'm not just thinking about it."

Harry tucked the letter inside the envelope and passed it back to Lee. "Why am I not surprised that you're behaving like this?"

"Like what?"

"Dramatically."

"What am I doing that's dramatic?"

"Crisscrossing the country with your draft letter, dramatic."

"You mean you think I'm cultivating drama?"

"That's what I mean I think."

"I'm not. It just *is* dramatic."

"You love it."

"I hate it."

"Please."

"Fuck you. What would you do?"

"I'd go, you fucking baby."

"You wouldn't."

"I would."

"Then why not enlist?"

"You're being evasive."

"I am or you are?"

"You are."

"*You* are."

"You're literally evading the draft."

"You're literally evading the question. Why don't you go down and enlist?"

"Maybe I will."

"Let's go right now."

"Maybe I will."

"Let's go."

"Maybe I will and maybe I won't."

This had been their style of communication for many years, but owing to their respective fatigue, or else the passage of time since their last meeting, it felt performative or re-enactive, and without the acrid contempt of their historic battles. When the argument petered out there came the question of how they might fill up the space of its absence. Harry stated that there were sixteen beers in the fridge, and he proposed that they should drink them. Lee demurred, explaining about the white crosses, describing his tiredness, and that he had to sleep. Harry countered that Lee could simply take more pills, and share some with himself. Afterward they could go to work on the beers, and what came next was anyone's guess. It hadn't occurred to Lee that he could skip a second cycle of sleep and was impressed with Harry's ingenuity, though he felt doubt that any number of pills would revive him. But he was game to try, and they ate one each, and within thirty minutes the drugs had taken hold and they were chatting animatedly and smoking many cigarettes as they made their progress against the beers. The morning passed pleasantly. Outside the house the day was coming on and Lee could hear music, voices, laughter, shouting. He asked Harry about this and Harry said it was always a party on the weekends. He stood and walked to the window and drew the curtains just enough to peer out. "All the houses in the neighborhood are owned by the factories, and they rent to the workers."

"What's that like?"

"Gets a little Wild West at times. Mostly things simmer here, but every once in a while they boil over." He turned to Lee. "How many beers've we got left?"

"None."

"I was afraid of that." Harry pointed out the window, at the world. "Want to go look around?"

Lee answered that he did, and they gathered themselves to go forth, both of them rumpled, unshaven, unclean. Soon the brothers were walking down the sidewalk together. They felt buoyant, and that no dark force was guiding them.

CRISIS NARRATIVES

THE AIR WAS HEAVY AND SLOW AND INTERESTING TO Lee. He was struck by the breadth of human activity taking place all around them. Each house they passed, it seemed that there were people going in or coming out, congregating on the porch or front steps, chatting away, shouting to one another from across the street, hailing cars as they drove by. Lee and Harry had been reared among hardened white faces, lipless, taciturn, inclined to wordless suspicion; now all around them were people of assorted backgrounds, and they were not hiding their feelings, and it was incongruous for Lee to see his brother walking among such lively citizens, and that he was one among them. People knew Harry, they called to him, he called back; a stylish Black man in sunglasses touched Harry's shoulder as he passed and asked how he was managing. Harry, not breaking stride, answered, "Badly!"

"Time'll take care of it," said the man.

"When?" asked Harry.

"In time," the man answered sensibly, and Harry saluted.

Lee said, "He knows your business?"

"Everyone knows everyone's business."

"And since when do you like people?"

Harry thought about this. "It's been about two years, now."

In the far corner of the sky there came a noise of turmoil and drumming, a small ball of thunder rolling overhead and away. Harry paused and squinted upward. He sat on a curb and began unlacing his shoes. Lee asked him what he was doing and Harry answered, "It's going to dump rain."

"So what?"

"So do what I do."

Lee sat down and gamely removed his sneakers. When Harry began peeling off his socks, Lee did the same. They put their socks into their shoes, their shoes into their back pockets, and resumed walking, but barefoot. They'd not made it to the end of the block before the rain began to fall: unique drops followed by the deluge, and people scattered to their homes, ducked under awnings and into storefronts. Harry and Lee were the only ones out, and this felt joyful, adventuresome. By the end of the next block the rain had let up and people were peering out from under dripping awnings, looking questioningly up at the sky. A minute or two later the streets and sidewalks were full again. Harry said, "Not far now."

"Where are we going?"

"Pyramids."

"What's Pyramids?"

"Bar I like."

"Should we put our shoes back on?"

"If we do that it'll only start raining again."

Lee saw a child of nine or ten years coming in their direction. He was carrying an apple crate, and his face read as one lost in troubling thought. When he saw Harry, however, his face softened; he walked up to block Harry's path and said, "So we meet again."

"Oh, hello Willie. What have you got there?"

"What's it look like?"

Harry rummaged the crate. "Milk and bread and other good things. Ice cream. Cigarettes. Were you just bringing all this to my house? You can leave it at the door; I'll pay you some other time, what do you think?"

"You're daydreaming."

"I do do that, it's true."

"And you smell like beer."

"Also true."

Willie set the crate on the sidewalk and looked at Lee, then back at Harry. In an answering tone, he said: "I got a job at McHenry's."

Harry was lighting a cigarette. "Moving up in the world, eh?" He took a long drag and exhaled. "Well, how do you like it?"

"Mr. McHenry's a hard man," Willie said. "But I like the delivery part. Being out in the world, seeing inside people's houses. See what they live like, you know?"

"Sure."

"See how they keep things, nice or messy?"

"Right."

"Because every place is different. And you never can know ahead of time whether somebody's going to be one way or the other." He paused. "I'll tell you this one thing: some people you wouldn't think are messy are messy. And some are *very* messy."

"Who are we talking about?"

Willie paused. "I don't think I should say."

"Professionalism," Harry said, nodding. "How's the wage?"

"Bad."

"You get tips?"

"Sometimes."

"You socking any away?"

"What I can."

"Saving up for what?"

"Haven't decided yet."

"You should get yourself a bike with a basket. That's twice the deliveries, twice the wage. You could turn that money around and make a killing in the stock market, what do you think?"

Willie was shaking his head. "The pay is flat rate." He looked again at Lee, asking Harry, "Who's this character?"

"This is my brother."

"You never said anything about a brother."

"I'm saying something about it now. Lee, this is Willie."

"Hi, Willie."

"Hello." Now Willie was looking at their feet. "Why aren't you men wearing your shoes?"

"Because we're going to Pyramids. And if there's one thing I can't stand it's drinking at Pyramids with wet feet."

"But your feet *are* wet."

"We'll dry them in Pyramids, then we'll slide into our dry socks and shoes and we'll have won the battle if not the war, see?"

"But you're wet everywhere else."

Harry told Lee, "Willie is one of the finest observers in the neighborhood."

"But what he's saying doesn't make sense," Willie told Lee. Now he became solemn, and said to Harry, "Look, though, hey, Harry? Hey, Harry? You don't want to go to Pyramids."

Harry drew his head up and back, as though he were looking down through bifocals, which lent him a magisterial air. "Sally's down there?"

"Down around there, yeah."

"Pyramids is my bar, Willie."

"Okay but I'm just telling you."

"You're telling me and I'm told and I thank you."

Willie said to Lee, "Oh, boy." He hefted his crate and continued in the direction he'd been going before stopping to chat. Lee and Harry walked in the opposite direction, and soon they arrived at Pyramids, a dank and dim place with a ratty pool table and an overall aura of misfortune. They sat at the bar, patting their feet with cocktail napkins and sliding into their dry socks and shoes. "Now, isn't that nice?" Harry asked, and it was nice, and Lee said that it was. They ordered beer from a bartender who seemed to be of two minds regarding Harry's character. When Harry asked him if Sally was around the bartender said she'd left ten minutes earlier, but that if she came back, he didn't want any trouble from Harry. In fact, he continued, he may well ask Harry to leave if she returned, and asked that Harry should do him a favor and prepare himself for that possibility. Harry drank the foam off his beer and said, "I'm prepared," then asked, "How's your mother?"

"She's been doing better."

"That's good."

"But then yesterday it got worse."

"That's bad."

"But now this morning she's getting better again."

"That's good."

"Thanks."

The bartender lingered and Harry said, "Great talking to you," and the bartender went away. Harry held up his beer. "How many does this make?"

"Nine apiece."

"And how many pills do we have left?"

"*I* have a bunch."

"Can *I* have one more?"

"Don't you feel the other one?"

"I feel the hell out of it." Harry held out his hand, and Lee tapped a pill into his palm, then one into his own, and they cheersed the pills, hopped them into their mouths, cheersed their beers, and washed the pills down. The bar was filling out as the post-lunchtime crowd arrived and the atmosphere grew richer and stranger. The Pyramids clientele was thirsty, raucous, a little vulgar; each of them was invested in their own momentary crisis narrative, just as Lee and Harry were invested in theirs. The brothers finished their round, then another; the alcohol began to stand up against the white crosses and they found themselves at the thrumming and emotionally various antechamber separating panic from sloth. It was not pleasant or unpleasant; certainly it was fascinating. Lee took a long breath and announced that he'd been angry at Harry for more than four years.

"You have?" said Harry. "Why?"

"Marinka."

"What about her? You weren't in love with her or some sickening thing, were you?"

"I think I was, yeah. Or anyway I liked her a lot."

Harry shrugged. "I didn't know you were a fan."

"You did know, though. And that's part of why you went after her, and that's part of what I've been angry about." Harry was listening with an expression of a man trying and failing to care; Lee further explained, "She had to leave town because of what you did to her."

"What I did to her," said Harry. "I'm sorry, have you convinced yourself that I did something to her she didn't want doing?" Lee didn't reply to this; bested, he looked importantly away. Harry was nodding, pointing. "That's right. Now let me tell you something else, Sir Sensitive Damsel-Saver. That girl hated Concrete. She hated the school, the town, the creeps she lived with, all of it. Who knows how it all shook out for her but I'll bet she landed in a better situation than the one she was in in Washington."

Lee listened and puzzled and wondered. He still could not absolve his brother of wrongdoing, as there was intent of malicious harm in his choosing Marinka as the object of his affections in the first place; but there *was* a sense of order to Harry's version of the story, and Lee believed it could be truer than his. He was not yet ready to let go of his own burnished reality all at once but thought it likely that forgiveness would come, over a period of hours or days, however long it took to turn one's ship around midsea.

Harry was flagging down the bartender. When the man approached, Harry asked, "Have you ever heard of the phenomenon of a barman serving his customers complimentary snacks? I'm told that it makes for a pleasant time."

The bartender said, "I've got your complimentary snack." He reached into his pants pocket, pulled out a middle finger. "Pig out, Harry."

Harry rested his chin in his palm, affecting a meditative mien: "When you were young, and all of life lay before you, did you one day sit up in your bed, gripped by the realization that you were destined to become a colorful area character?"

"I've got your colorful area."

"Don't stop now, neighbor, you're on a hot streak."

"I've got your hot streak."

Lee was only half listening to this when he became distracted by a woman sitting farther down the bar. She was an attractive girl in her early twenties drinking a schooner of beer and she looked to be in good spirits, perhaps somewhat drunk. When Lee caught her eye she smiled impishly, then held up her hand in such a way as to say: watch! She took an ashtray from the bar, carefully and thoroughly emptying its contents into her near-full beer. Next she stood away from her stool and marched toward Lee. Her smile was the same as before, only its context had changed, so that Lee understood something unpleasant was going to happen, and then it did: the woman approached Harry from behind, raised the glass, and slowly poured her dirty beer over his head. As the clumpy gray-black liquid drew down Harry's face in rivulets he sat frozen, mouth agape, both hands held out stiffly before him, a mannequin in distress. After the woman emptied the glass, she set it on the bar and made for the exit. This beer-pouring action had caught the attention of the other patrons, many of whom erupted in hearty applause, and the woman turned with a flourish as she opened the door, waving like a dignitary before vanishing into the rectangle of bright afternoon sunlight. The door swung shut, the bar returned to darkness, the applause faded away, and the bartender, smiling, held out a towel for Harry. "Sally?" Harry asked, and the bartender nodded and said, "Sally." He went away and Harry took out a comb and began styling his hair, picking away the cigarette butts from the comb's tines. The entire incident resembled more performed ritual than occurrence of assault in public and Harry, after a moment of introspection, said that he accepted what had happened as passably fair according to the laws of commonsensical justice. "Tit for tat, the ancient currency," he said wonderingly.

They drank two more beers each; Harry became expansive. He said that he felt he was looking at his biography from a great remove, all of his experience laid out to be regarded as a solitary mass. He gripped Lee's forearm; in an urgent tone, he said, "Do you want to know what's wrong with me? It's that I *like* to make things turn bad. I *like* it when I get to spoil things."

"Other people's things."

"No, let's be fair about it, it's my things too. Some awful part of me is thrilled at the mess I've made of my own life." Harry was looking at himself in the mirror behind the bar. "What does it mean that I feel this way? Does it point to a deficiency of heart?"

"Yes," said Lee.

"Okay, but does it?" Harry seemed doubtful, and began a rambling monologue aimed in the direction of bestowing blame not upon himself but upon their experience of childhood, upon the town of Concrete, or what he called the spirit behind the town of Concrete, which he described as a bleak specter, corruptive, lesser-making. Lee did not recognize the theory as meaningful or true but Harry was impassioned and did not need his brother's support. He was working toward a crescendo of some sort, and Lee became intrigued when he understood he was to be a witness to the confession of a secret truth. He encouraged Harry to identify whatever it was, but just as Harry arrived at the precipice, he demurred. "If I just say it, then it's over."

"What's over?"

"The moment of me naming what it is that I do."

"What you do?"

"The thing I do."

"You do a thing?"

"That's right. Look, wait here and I'll show you, okay?" Harry walked across the barroom to the pay phone. He made a brief call, looking blankly at Lee while he spoke. When he returned, he began gathering his effects from the bar. "We're leaving," he said.

"What's going on?"

"You'll see when we get there." He called for the bill, received it, and passed it to Lee. Lee paid and they exited the bar, starting off for downtown, with Harry leading the way.

"Just tell me what we're doing," said Lee.

"If I tell you, then you're technically an accessory."

"Accessory to what?"

Harry turned a key in his mouth and threw it away over his shoulder. In the distance there came the plaintive wow of a fire engine's siren; Harry snapped and pointed at his ear. Then more sirens, more snapping and pointing.

Ambulances and police cars roared past and the brothers were shuffled into a growing body of curious citizens likewise seeking out the source of the disruption. Entering Duluth's Civic Center, they found city hall in a state of chaos: firemen unspooling their hoses, policemen running around, news vans clogging the area and jockeying for space, and the marshal standing at the midpoint of the grand concrete stairwell leading to the building's entrance, speaking urgently into a bullhorn that all should *continue moving, maintain calm, the area must be cleared.* To the side of the marshal a long line of harried-looking men and women in suits and skirts was being led down the stairwell by a policeman who held his billy club above his head, as a tour guide hoists a flag to mark his location. A barricade stood at the base of the stairwell and newscasters crowded the sidewalk in a line, staring into the lenses of behemoth cameras and delivering their collected informations with grave resignation.

Lee asked Harry, "Sorry, what was the phone call?"

"Bomb threat," Harry answered. "Shall we sit?"

Harry and Lee sat on a bench in the square and watched the evacuation of city hall. Harry looked proud, as one receiving an earned entertainment. Once the building had been emptied there came the time of waiting, policemen and firemen standing at a remove, checking their watches, the red lights of their vehicles swiveling silently.

"What do you say when you call?" Lee asked.

"It depends. Today I said, 'Hello, I've planted a bomb in city hall and it's going to explode at the top of the hour.'" He looked at his watch. "Two minutes, watch, everyone gets all small and serious." The assembled crowd of uniformed men took their defensive positions, hiding behind their vehicles, mailboxes. The top of the hour came and went. Slowly and by degrees, the men stood, looked about. The marshal returned to the midpoint of the stairwell and resumed his monologue into the bullhorn, but now he was stating *the area was safe, all should return to their stations, the threat was passed, thank you for your cooperation and have a nice day.* His free hand came up in a gesture of speech-giving emphasis and Lee thought he looked like a performer on the stage of an epic opera, or a figurine on the face of a cake. The professional men and women of city hall trudged back up the stairs in scattered twos and threes and Harry sat watching his brother with an expression describing self-satisfaction.

"So?" he asked.

"So what?"

"So what do you think?"

"About your new hobby?"

"Yeah."

Lee said, "I think you might be suffering some kind of emotional disintegration and that you're almost certainly going to go to prison."

Harry shook his head, his face puckering in disgust. "I knew you wouldn't get it."

"I don't get it."

"You admit you don't get it."

"I'm admitting I don't, yeah." Lee paused. "Would you like to explain it to me?"

Harry gestured at the scene before them. "I did this, you know? I created this atmosphere. When was the last time you created an atmosphere?"

"I don't think that I've ever created an atmosphere."

"Well, how could you understand, then?" Harry sighed. "Sometimes," he said, "you see someone who's convinced they're about to get blown to pieces, and their terror is very interesting. Or you'll see a cop or fireman, and he's huffing and puffing, running around thinking he's some pure hero, you know? He's having his big moment, and later he's going to tell his buddies about it, his neighbors, his poor goddamned wife."

"And why do these things please you?"

"Humanity's moronic parade, Lee. And then there's the dessert aspect of it, which is that these people are feeling these feelings for no reason—all the extremes played out on behalf of nothing. I wouldn't enjoy it if I actually planted a bomb."

"Wouldn't you?"

"Of course not. None of it's real, that's the point."

"But the panic is real."

"It's real but it's not true."

"It's true for the people experiencing it."

"What exactly is the nature of your critique, here?"

"I'd call it a critique of time management. But also that it's unfriendly."

"I freely admit that it's unfriendly." Harry thought. "Do you think what you're doing to America is friendly?"

"What I'm doing to America?"

"Walking out on her?"

"Her?"

"It's unfriendly."

"Going to Vietnam is friendly?"

The barricade was being dismantled by two phlegmatic policemen. Harry said, "Look, don't spoil this for me, all right? It's all I've got going on right now." Lee was surprised by the hurt tone in Harry's voice. He saw that Harry had made himself vulnerable by exposing his private pastime, and now, in light of Lee's response, felt himself unfairly judged, misunderstood. "And don't tell Mom," he added, and Lee said he wouldn't.

They drifted back to Harry's house, neither of them having much to say to the other. Harry retired to his room and Lee slept on the couch. In the morning Harry was sick and Lee wasn't, and Lee was glad, but Harry also was glad, because he had met the day with the pain of self-pitying sorrow, which in connection with the pain of his hangover made him feel that he was pain through and through, and this gave him a sense of purpose.

Lee stood at the bathroom door listening to his brother's driven retching. There came a lull and Lee knocked and Harry said, "Go away," and Lee entered. Harry was sitting on the floor, wedged in between the toilet and the bathtub, attempting to connect the flame of his lighter with the end of his cigarette with one eye shut. Upon succeeding, he took a meditative drag, then flushed the toilet. "Illustrate the scene with Dad for me," he said.

Lee shook his head. "Too awful."

"Small illustration," said Harry.

Lee shrugged. "He's poorly."

"His health is poorly?"

"Yeah, but it's more that his life is not, you know, overburdened by grace."

"He's poorly in the spiritual sense," Harry said.

"He is suffering from spiritual poverty," Lee agreed.

"His spirituality is down on its luck."

"He's dissolving. Right now I'd say he's about two-thirds gone, and the third third's going fast."

"Maybe you caught him on a bad day."

"I don't think so."

The toilet was running; Harry reached his right hand up over his left shoulder and jiggled the handle. He took a deep and energizing breath. "You think he's got any money in the bank, or insurance policies? Sometimes these old hermit type of birds, you know, they have it socked away in bales."

Lee said, "You really do have a lousy personality there, don't you?"

As one conceding a point, Harry said, "I have a lot of bad feelings."

"You think that's all there is to it?"

"Anyway, it's a big part of it. What am I supposed to do? The thoughts that come are the ones that come." He tried to get up but was stuck. "I'm in this hole, here," he said, and held out his hand. Lee helped his brother up and they repaired to the kitchen. Harry made himself a bowl of raisin bran, sat at the table, and stared at it. "I can't eat this." Lee sat and commenced eating the cereal. "Why are you dunning everyone for money?" he asked, chewing. "I thought the steel factory paid a mint."

"It's not a bad job, and that's the truth. I just can't seem to hold on to the money once I get it."

"Where's it go?"

"Things and things."

"What things?"

Harry cleared his throat. "Things like, I bought a horse and it died after two and a half days, right?"

"Right," Lee said.

"Then I sued the ex-owner after I realized he'd sold me a horse that he knew was dying. And he really did know, too—but he also knew the judge. So not only did I not get reimbursed for the dead horse, but I had to pay the guy I bought the dead horse from's lawyer fees, on top of my own. The final insult came from the crematorium. The man called me up and said, 'We'll be holding on to your horse's ashes until the bill is settled.' I said, 'Let me explain where I want you to put my horse's ashes.'" He paused. "Does Mom or Uncle Wallace have any money?"

"Doesn't seem like it."

Shaking his head, he said, "I cannot fucking believe that I'm carless."

Lee, smiling, said, "You haven't a car in the world."

"Stop."

"You couldn't car less."

"Shut up!" Harry thought a moment. His face brightened and he said, "Hey, how about a pill for the road?"

"I'm going on the road. You're staying in the house."

"How about a pill for the house?"

Lee counted out two pills. Harry took his with tap water, Lee with the last of the milk from the cereal bowl. He stood and set the bowl in the sink. "Wash the bowl," said Harry. Lee washed the bowl and set it on the rack to dry. Harry asked if he could borrow some money and Lee said he couldn't. They shook hands and felt embarrassed about it and Lee drove away thinking about the oddments of the story of the day: he had seen his brother and found him in pain, and the pain had humanized him, and Lee had enjoyed Harry for the first time since they were children. Lee felt certain his brother's future held some ghastly comeuppance but he couldn't deny that in the meantime Harry wore his freakish proportions with panache. The most powerful monster of all, Lee decided, was the monster in possession of style.

PLUMMETING MOMENTS OF TERROR AND ABHORRENCE

LEE DROVE FOR ELEVEN HOURS AND CHECKED INTO A motor lodge on the edge of Columbus, Ohio. He spoke haltingly to the clerk; his brain felt warm and he found himself reaching for plain words that weren't there. He had taken too many drugs for too many successive days and this had created a void in his mind, and when he blinked he could see clusters of tiny white explosions at the edge of his field of vision, pinpricks of light that he found troubling and fascinating in equal measure.

His room was clean but meager, with a paper bath mat and half-size towels. He took a shower and lay on the creaking, listing bed but couldn't sleep, agitated by the belief that something, he wasn't sure what, needed doing. He dressed and made for the phone booth out front of the manager's office. It was a cool night, and pretty; Lee dialed Cal's number with the accordion door half open. It rang twenty times and an operator came on to tell Lee his party was not at home. She disconnected the call and Lee dialed again and let it ring twenty more times and a different operator disconnected him. Lee placed a third call and a man picked up after ten rings. "Fuck, man, what?" he said.

Lee shut the accordion door. "Robin?"

Robin, sheepish: "Oh, hey Lee. How's it going."

Lee made to collect himself. "How's it going," he repeated. But he didn't answer the question because he didn't know what the answer was.

Robin said, "I guess you're probably wondering what I'm doing at Cal's place, huh?"

"Yes, I'm wondering that," Lee said.

"Well, do you want to hear the whole thing or part of it or none of it or what?"

"Might as well hear the whole thing."

"The truth?"

"Let's go for the truth, yeah."

"Okay." Robin cleared his throat. "I'd like to start at the start, or before, even, and by pointing out the obvious, which is that you'd have to be a eunuch not to notice Cal, do you know what I mean?"

"Yes."

"And I'm not a eunuch, and I did notice. But she was your old lady and I swear to God I never once put out the most minuscule exploratory amorous vibration."

"All right."

"I'm being very serious with you right now, Lee."

"Yeah."

"But then you were gone. And she says you're not coming back, and she's not the kind of girl to stay single for long. So then comes the imperative, right?"

"Right."

"Nobody invites the imperative. The imperative arrives of its own accord. It has arrived, and there you go, you know? There you are."

"Okay, but who came around, her or you?"

"I came around."

"Knocked on her door?"

"I alerted Cal of my presence by knocking on the door, yeah."

"Then what?"

"She answered?"

"Then what?"

"I came in?"

"How did you come in?"

"Right foot left foot, man. What are you talking about?"

"But did she invite you in?"

"Yes!"

"*How* did she invite you in?"

"She said, 'Oh, hey, what's up Robin, come in.'" He'd imitated her lazy drawl, so that Lee could see her face speaking the words.

"And then what?" Lee asked.

"Then whatever."

"Not whatever."

"What do you want me to tell you?"

"Tell me what happened."

"Why?"

"Say it so I know what's real."

Robin sighed. "We smoked a joint and drank some mai tais and screwed on the floor, all right?"

A ringing gathered in Lee's ears. "What, on the pillows?"

"Yeah, why? Are those your special pillows or something?"

"I guess I'd thought they were my special pillows, yeah."

"Well, what the fuck," said Robin. "I didn't know that. How was I supposed to know that? Jesus Christ!"

"Jesus Christ," Lee agreed.

"Do you want me to keep going, or should I stop?"

"Keep going."

"Okay, keeping going. And the worst part's over, just so you know."

"Great."

"It's after, and we're sitting around drinking the last of the mai tais and listening to some records and I asked Cal about her plans for the rest of the day. She says she's got nothing doing, just that she needed to go to the Wash-N-Whirl. So I offer to drive her. Okay, she says. And I take her and her laundry over there."

"In my car."

"Your former old lady in your former car, yeah. Does that bug you?"

"Yes."

"Well, I think it bugged her too. I guess she'd forgotten that I'd bought it from you? She sort of froze when she saw it, you know?"

"Uh-huh. Then what?"

"Then she unfroze, and we got in the car and we're driving, not talking. And I don't know what she was thinking about but what I was thinking about was what had just happened between she and me, and what it meant, as in what it amounted to. And by the time we pulled up at the Wash-N-Whirl I was plotting out the rest of our lives together, more or less. Sorry, Lee, but that's how it hit me."

"Over the moon."

"Way over it, yeah, and in a way that felt very crazy, very not normal. But I'm going to play it cool because that's what Cal's doing, and that's what the situation calls for, and I say to her, in a casual tone, 'Maybe I'll stick around and keep you company while you do your laundry.' But Cal shakes her head, no. 'You don't want me to stick around?' She shakes her head. She was being spooky and hiding behind her hair that way she does sometimes, you know what I mean?"

"Yeah."

"And the whole thing sets me back on my heels a bit, because I'm not used to caring so much. And I'm definitely not used to not getting my way when it comes to girls, and so I say to myself, buddy? Play it even cooler. 'Okay then, see you around, Cal,' and I drive off with the radio blaring like I don't give a shit. But I *do* give a shit. And I *don't* see her around. So I start dropping by her apartment, more or less hourly, but she's never home. Then I'm leaving notes, remind her what my number is—nothing. Now it's been days of looking for her and other than one short and horrible phone call there's no sign of her and I feel like I've slipped into some fucked-up little pit, here, and I'm not sleeping hardly at all and I don't know what I'm doing half the time, more than half the time."

Lee was shaking his head. "Okay, but how bad can it be if you're at her place, you know?"

"What?"

"You're acting like I should feel sorry for you, but you guys have obviously worked it out or you wouldn't be over there, right?"

"No, sorry, wait a minute—you're not understanding what's going on here, Lee."

"What's going on?"

"She's not around right now," Robin said carefully. "Do you know what I mean by that?"

"I don't, no."

"I mean she's not here. And she doesn't know I'm here, either."

Lee asked, "You broke into Cal's apartment?"

"I think I might have."

"You think you might have?"

"Yeah."

"But what happened, you came by and she wasn't there?"

"Yeah."

"You tried the door?"

"Tried it."

"Was it locked or unlocked?"

"What?"

"Was the door locked or unlocked?"

"Let's say I unlocked it," Robin answered, and paused. "I know, Lee, okay? I know what you're thinking and I know that you're right but I have to have some forward motion on this or I'm going to do something desperate."

"More desperate."

"More desperate."

"How long have you been there?"

"I broke in right around this time last night."

"And you slept over?"

"Spent the night. Have not slept."

"Not at all?"

"No."

"Hard time?"

"Hard time." He said he hadn't planned to stay over, but entering the apartment by force had set a precedent. "If the door'd been unlocked, I probably would have left after five minutes. But now I'm suddenly the love burglar, right? And I had to see this thing through to its sickening conclusion. So I settle in, take a couple pills, smoke twenty cigarettes in a row, watch a little TV. Drink some delicious fucking tap water, you know what I mean?"

"Uh-huh."

"I was waiting for the bars to close."

"Right."

"Two o'clock comes and goes. Well, okay, sometimes it takes a minute to get home. Three o'clock, no Cal. Somehow it hadn't occurred to me that she might not come home but now I'm realizing that's a possibility or probability. And I started to wonder if it wasn't a great idea to kick out every one of the windows in the apartment."

"Losing it."

"Close to losing it, yeah. But then I went home instead."

"But now you're back."

"I've been dipping in and out all day."

"Right."

Robin paused. "You understand she's in another man's bed, Lee, right?"

"Yeah, I got that," Lee said. "Whose do you think it is?"

"Not sure. But I know it's been going on for the last few days."

"How do you know that?"

"The short and horrible phone call."

"Which was what?"

"I got her on the line for one hot second, asked if there was another guy, and she said there was and I told her, 'Just give me the motherfucker's name.' You know what she said to me? She said, 'You already know his name. And you know he's not a motherfucker.'"

"Huh," said Lee.

"Huh is right," said Robin. "Two clues, and one as useless as the next. Because for one, I know more than half the people in this town, and for two, if you think about it, and I've been thinking about it a lot, very few people are motherfuckers."

"Yeah."

"The true motherfucker is a rare thing. So it could be anyone, really. I thought it was Shoobie, but it's not."

"Who's Shoobie?"

"You know Shoobie. Sells shells at the swap meet?"

"I don't know him."

"Well, it's not him."

"Why'd you think it was?"

"No real reason, actually. I just really didn't want it to be him."

"Why?"

"Shoobie's the guy you don't want it to be, Lee, trust me. Which isn't to say he's a motherfucker, because he's not."

"Right. So, now you're just sitting around until she comes home?"

"That's the plan."

"And what if she brings the new beau?"

"Then somebody's going to get their fucking lights punched out."

"What if he punches out yours?"

"Then that's what he'll do. Either way I'll have some clarity."

"Right." Lee paused. "Have you thought about what Cal's response to all this is going to be?"

"Yes, I have. And I think she's going to be severely pissed at me."

"Yeah."

"You think so too?"

"Yes."

"You think I should go?"

"I don't know what anyone should do."

"Well, I guess I'll figure it out," said Robin. "Hey, though, how's everything going with you? You make it to Canada?"

"No, I'm in Ohio."

"How are the zoomers?"

"The what?"

"The white crosses."

"Oh, they're good."

"They'll zoom you."

"Yeah, I'm zoomed."

"You sleeping?"

"Some."

"You eating?"

"Not much."

"You gotta make yourself eat."

"Okay."

"How's that Jag?"

"It's good."

"Just good?"

"It's great."

"How's the family?"

"Great."

"That's good," said Robin. Then: "Hey, Lee? Look, I'm sorry, seriously."

"Yeah."

"I mean it. This was a fucked-up thing to do to you—though I didn't do it on purpose."

"You did."

"Okay, but I feel bad about it."

"Right."

"Though I'd do it again if I could."

"Sure," said Lee.

"Can I say that I'm impressed with how you're taking this?" Robin said, brightening. "I thought you'd be way more mad about it."

"If it were going better I think I would be."

"More mad?"

"Yeah."

"It's going pretty bad," Robin admitted.

"Yeah. And I won't say good luck."

"But no hexing?"

"No hexing."

"Cool, man. Okay, see you around. Or not. You know what I mean."

Lee said he did know, and hung up the phone. There was a fried chicken restaurant on the far side of the highway and he crossed over and took a seat at the counter. He wasn't hungry but ordered steak and eggs, and as he ate he thought of the many hours he'd spent with Cal at the Wash-N-Whirl, of her transferring damp clothes from a washer to a dryer, the bottoms of her bare feet dirty, legs unimpeachable, and the way she turned a chore into a game, a glad performance in the midst of tedium. She often spoke of what she had called real-time sportsmanship, which was her theory that one should approach even the most banal aspects of life with an attitude of being in play. Lee remembered the time when, partway through the first of several wash cycles, Cal lost a two-of-three Rochambeau, and per their agreement had to do Lee's bidding. When he announced that he wanted a margarita Cal did not hesitate but glided to the pay phone, called a taxi, and moved to stand barefoot at the curb. The taxi came quickly and she was away; ten minutes later the taxi returned and Cal emerged, pitcher held high, smile of triumph lighting up her pretty, proud face. Having no cups, they drank from the pitcher. It was eleven o'clock in the morning and with the onset of drunkenness, there came to Lee the sense that this was all life had to be to be considered prosperous.

He returned to his room at the motor lodge. He stripped and got into bed and lay in the dark, his mind crowded with indignities. After thirty minutes he knew that he wouldn't sleep, and decided to leave, to drive through the night to New York, where he would sit and speak with his sister, who understood him, and whom he understood, and together they would make sense of things, or else commit to the idea that there would be no making sense, that life was not meant to add up to any one round sum. He dressed and took a pill and packed and stowed his suitcase in the Jaguar. He stopped at the first gas station he came across and bought six beers and a pack of cigarettes. He drove and drank and smoked and in thirty minutes his unfriendly mood had been replaced with a sense of strength, resilience. He turned on the radio, landing on a rock-and-roll station, and the music perfectly re-created his emotional reality: fearless belligerence with deep psychic panic operating at the perimeter. He turned the radio all the way up, the music shrieking and trebly, rattling the speakers in the door panels. Lee Clarke drove through the night to New York City at an even eighty, experiencing pulsing surges of deranged happiness followed by plummeting moments of terror and abhorrence.

INTERESTING THINGS

GRACE'S APARTMENT BUILDING WAS A CRUMBLING prewar affair, sooty brick and dirty windows, laundry strung out on the fire escape. It was ten o'clock in the morning; Lee climbed four flights of stairs, faces peering out at him as he stepped past, and they were not lucky faces. Lee knocked on Grace's door and she answered, horrified at the sight of him. "What happened?"

"I'm ahead of schedule."

"But what happened?"

"What do you mean?"

She led him to the bathroom mirror to show him what he looked like.

"I'm tired," he said.

"You're embalmed."

"I need to sleep."

"You can sleep all day, but talk to me while I get ready for work. There's some interesting things I want to tell you."

He followed her to the kitchen, watching her heating up cold coffee in a blackened saucepan on a hot plate resting on a shaky wooden crate. The apartment was dark, cramped, uncomfortable, and unclean. "Nice place," Lee said.

"I know it's a dump, but I like the neighborhood. And I love living alone." She set the steaming saucepan of burned coffee on the table.

Lee asked, "What are the interesting things?"

Grace was pouring the coffee into a chipped enamel mug. "Just that my life is a very thrilling adventure at the moment."

"You've got the doctor in the bag?"

"The trash bag."

"What?"

"The doctor's chapter is in the ancient past, Lee."

"You're not sad about it?"

"I'm waving my kerchief at it from the caboose of the train. But I'm not sad, no, and I have no idea where all those huge feelings went but thank God they're gone. All of a sudden, Lee, I *saw* him. And he was this chinless, slope-shouldered, jiggle-titted peeve."

"What do you think prompted the clarity?"

"Claude, Claude," she said.

"Who's Claude, Claude?"

"He's the man I've been looking for all my life."

"Where'd you meet him?"

"At the hospital."

"Pitting doctor against doctor?"

"Claude is not a doctor."

"I suppose he's a patient," said Lee drolly.

"As a matter of fact, he is," Grace stated.

"Claude, Claude is crazy?"

"Sometimes."

"What kind of crazy?"

"Traditional madman. Foaming at the mouth, speaking in tongues, murderous urge. Then comes the scrum of orderlies, the straitjacket, sedation, isolation."

"How often does this happen?"

"Every four or five weeks."

"And what's he like in between episodes?"

"Dynamic. Passionate. Quicksilver mind. Hardish to follow. Intense but tender, never angry."

Lee said, "I don't understand how all this happened in so short a time."

"Oh, the Claude thing's been building for months. He started in around February—twenty-eight days of long stares. March was a lot of standing-close-as-often-as-possible-coincidentally, with emanating waves of humid lust pulsing back and forth between us. April into May it was the stares and close-standing with the added occasional brief physical contact that felt like being burned deliciously with a hot iron. Finally, day before yesterday, I could tell something was different, like he'd made up his mind. He followed me around the ward all morning, then I went into the storeroom, left the door open. The door that locks from the inside. And I think you can guess the rest."

"Wow."

"Wow is right. Have you ever made love to a lunatic?"

"I haven't."

"I'm not saying you should seek it out, but if the opportunity ever arises, I can vouch for the experience." Grace took a thoughtful sip of coffee. "Did I mention that he's completely and utterly beautiful? Like Christ with a gym membership?"

"That's nice."

"It's more than nice."

"Is he funny?"

"No sense of humor whatsoever. As in, none."

"All business."

"But in a noble way."

"When he's not insane."

Grace nodded. "His approach to life is severe, but he doesn't drag his feet or pity himself. It's like he comes from an ancient time, before jokes were invented."

"And what does the good doctor think about all this?"

"He doesn't know, at least not factually. But he must sense my having moved on, because I can hardly keep up with the declarations of undying love. The human heart is a sick organ."

"Poor the good doctor."

"He'll be fine. There are new interns pouring in daily, each with two tits apiece. And he's got that bovine at home, don't forget, chewing her cud and mooing over the goblin-child."

"I didn't know about the goblin-child."

"Unparalleled goblin."

"There you go, then," Lee said. "And what comes next? Think you and Claude'll settle down, pick out a nice padded room together, have some crazy babies?"

"No, but we are planning on doing some stand-up screwing in the boiler room during quiet time this afternoon." Grace looked at her watch. "Why don't you get some sleep and I'll be back around dinnertime. What do you want to do tonight?"

"What do you normally do?"

"Walk, talk, eat, and drink." She moved to the door, paused, turned, her hand on her hip. "I just have the feeling that I want to flush my entire life down the toilet, do you understand?"

"I do understand. I mean, that's what I'm doing."

Grace smiled. She hadn't thought of it, and it pleased

her. "Take a shower before you get in my bed, all right? No offense, but you stink." Lee gave the OK sign and Grace left, humming to herself as she walked down the stairs.

Lee got in the shower and sat down in the stall. The hot water was soothing against his weary flesh, and he promptly fell asleep. When the hot water ran out, the cold woke him up in a state of expansive alarm. He toweled off and sought out Grace's bed, a mattress on the floor next to a cast iron radiator coated in many layers of paint. He slept for nine hours; Grace woke him up by shaking his shoulder. She had a wild look in her eye and she told Lee, "I was fired! Meet me in the kitchen and I'll tell you every single thing!" She dashed from the bedroom and began banging around in the kitchen. Lee followed after and found her sitting at the wobbly little table drinking a can of beer. He asked her what had happened and she said, "Remember Claude and me and the boiler room? Well, we got caught."

Lee grimaced. "How caught?"

"As caught as two people can be, that's how caught we got."

"Who caught you?"

"Claude had me up against the wall when the good doctor barged in."

"Barged in and then what?"

"Pitched a general fit. Stomping up and down in his

size fives, waving his arms around, yelling at us to get dressed, which we did, and which he watched. Once the show was over he stormed off, sent in the orderlies to get Claude, who was standing there with tented pants, and the orderlies trying not to laugh about it as they led him away. I was buckling my shoes when Miss Mosely came in all haughty and triumphant. She never did like me, not from the start."

"Who's Miss Mosely?"

"Boss nurse, big pig, big shithead. Called me a fly-by-nighter when I first came to the ward and I guess she was right about that, not that it matters. Anyway, I wanted to get at the good doctor but he was hiding in his office, and Miss Mosely was barring the way, so we had a bit of a thing in the hallway."

"A bit of a thing."

"Bit of a wresting exhibition."

"Like rolling around on the floor?"

"No, she just sort of bear-hugged me, smothering me with her huge tits."

"What were you going to say to him?"

"The good doctor? Honestly, I was just going to go for him."

"Attack him?"

"Yeah."

Lee was impressed. "I don't think I've ever seen you angry like that."

"I've never been anywhere *near* that angry before, Lee, not in my life." She sipped her beer. "It's scary to think of now, actually; because I really wasn't in control of myself. I guess that's how people get murdered occasionally, right? Passion killing?"

"That's one of the ways. Can I have a beer?"

"There's only this one."

"Can I have a sip?"

Grace passed Lee her beer and he took a sip and handed it back. "So Miss Mosely bear-hugs you until what?"

"Until I calmed down, which took a few minutes. Finally she asked if I was ready to be civil and I said I was, and she unclenched me, and I waited a beat, then made to get around her and bolt down the hall. She grabbed me by the wrist, swung me around like a Lindy dancer, hauled off and slapped me a good one." Grace pointed at her cheek. "Is there a mark?"

"It's red, yeah."

Grace touched her face gingerly. "I'll tell you something, it's shocking to be slapped like that. But I guess she meant to bring me to heel, and it worked perfectly—I was an angel afterward. She followed me to the cloakroom to get my purse and sweater, then the orderlies walked me down. As in, escorted me from the building. Not that they were nasty about it. They were still pretty amused by the whole thing. One told the other, 'This little lady has had an up and down day.'" Grace lit a cigarette. "Have you been sleeping this whole time?"

"Yeah."

"Feeling better?"

"I'm still tired."

"Want to sleep more?"

"No."

"Want to go out?"

"Sure. Are we commiserating or celebrating?"

"Neither. Both. Commiserbrating. Get dressed."

Lee got dressed and met Grace in the bathroom. She'd changed into a denim skirt and a man's work shirt and her hair was up and she was inspecting her cheek. Lee looked drawn in the glare of the too-bright lightbulb; Grace looped her arm around his, and they stood studying themselves and each other in the mirror. "Look at this pair of madcaps," said Grace.

"Life is beating us up."

"It is, isn't it?" She put her head on her brother's shoulder. "You still stink."

"I need to wash my clothes."

"We'll stop at a laundromat on the way to the bar."

Lee tied two shirts together at the sleeves, fashioning a bindle to carry the dirty clothes. He took a white cross and offered Grace one and she took it and asked what it was. They left the apartment and walked down the stairs, laughing slightly, but not about any one thing, just that they were together and in novel circumstances. When Lee had arrived that morning there weren't very many people about but now he and Grace had to walk in the street to avoid the crowd on the sidewalk. Clubs and coffeehouses and playhouses and bookstores, all filled with bodies streaming in and out—Sunday night in Greenwich Village. Lee asked Grace where they were going. "There's a bar I went to last winter, hole in the wall where all the lefty heavies hang out."

"Lefty heavies."

"Yeah."

"And why are we going there?"

"I'm looking for someone."

"Who?"

"Guy who took me there's name is Chucky. He's a big wheel with the COs and draft resistance people. I thought it might be good for you to meet him."

Lee grimaced. "Can't we just get drunk instead?"

"We can do both things," Grace said. She pointed. "There's the laundromat. I'll wait out here."

The laundromat was empty save for a wino sitting in the corner and reading a newspaper with a studious expression. Lee put a load in, then looked around for a manager. He wanted to speak with someone about leaving his laundry unattended, but the office door was locked and there was no one around. Thinking the wino might be there in some semiofficial capacity, Lee asked, "Sir, do you work here?"

The wino's voice was clear, earnest: "No, I'm not currently employed."

"Well do you think it'd be all right if I leave my laundry here while I have a beer up the street?"

"I think that would be perfectly fine," answered the wino. He rattled his paper and returned to his reading, the paper obscuring his upper half, now. Crossing his legs, he exposed a sockless ankle, monstrously swollen from his shin and to the top of the foot. The flesh was wet and rotted-looking and his lower pant leg had been ripped at the inseam to allow for the ankle's unnatural girth. Lee noticed, only after a lengthy study of the man's condition, that there were eyeholes cut from the paper, and that the wino was watching him. Grace called from the sidewalk and Lee hurried off, grateful for the exit cue, but sensing the man's gaze following him until he was away and out of sight.

Grace led Lee down an alley reeking of trash and urine. They came to a much-abused metal door with no signage and entered a dim bar, airless, and no music was playing. The room was three-fourths full, dour, gray faces turning to watch Lee and Grace. Grace sat in a booth and Lee went to the bar for beers, stopping at a pay phone on the way, dialing Cal's number: no answer. He tried to make conversation with the bartender but the bartender wouldn't indulge him. The faces lining the bar all regarded him with cold suspicion. He moved to the booth with two pints. "Fun crowd," he said.

"Who'd you call?"

"Cal."

"Not home?"

"Never home."

"Do you want to talk about her?"

"There's nothing to talk about. Everything's shitty."

"Shitty how?"

Lee told her about the phone call with Robin. Grace, solemn: "A buddy-fucker. That's tough, Lee."

"I know. It's giving me hard feelings about her."

"So it's all over."

"It was already over. But now the past feels spoiled, too. Like it didn't mean to her what it meant to me."

Grace considered this. "That doesn't have to be true," she said. "Also it doesn't have to be over. She sounds a little fancy-free, but maybe she's acting out to get away from the feeling of your being gone. You left her, remember."

"She could have come."

"You invited her?"

"She knows she could have come."

"Uh-huh."

"What?"

Grace took a long sip of her beer. "It's not enough that you expect her to want to completely upend her life, her home, her school and friendships, she's supposed to beg you to do it."

"You think I'm being a dick?"

Grace said, "I think you're being somewhat of a dick."

They finished their first round, and then a second. Lee returned to the laundromat to transfer his clothes to the dryer but when he got there he found that someone had done this for him, socks and underwear hopping around in a dryer's portal window. What did this mean? The wino with the monster ankle was gone, his paper folded neatly on the chair. There were thirty minutes left on the dryer cycle and Lee returned to the bar. Grace had fetched a third round; Lee took a sip of his beer and asked, "What are you going to do about Claude?"

"What's to do? Nothing."

"But you won't be able to see him again, right?"

Grace shook her head.

"You're not upset about it?"

She shrugged.

"The man you've been looking for all your life, you said."

"Well, it's fun, talking like that. And within the realm of the ward he was the catch of the day, absolutely. But what am I supposed to do, wait in chastity for his release? And when he's out, then what? I take him to the movies, watch him attack the popcorn lady?" Grace shook her head. "I'll tell you what I *am* upset about," she said.

"What."

"What I *am* upset about is that Harvey's getting away with what he's getting away with."

"Who's Harvey?"

"The good doctor."

"Harvey?"

"That's his name."

"What's Harvey getting away with?"

She pulled a cigarette from her pack and tapped it on the tabletop. "I put up with that amoeba's needs for half the year and now he just gets to set me to the side?"

"You're saying you want him back?"

"No, just that I want him to suffer." She lit her cigarette and smoked awhile. "When he caught me with Claude today, he was the wounded lover, and his eyes showed me real pain. But then the wheels started turning, and in a minute I could see that he was thinking: *no, this is the answer to the problem of her. Now I can send her away and be done with it.* And look, that's just what he did, right? Bull's-eye." She looked at Lee expectantly. "Well?"

"Well what?"

"What should I do about my bad feelings?"

"I don't know. What can you do?"

She thought about it. As one being swept up in a gathering wonder, she said, "I could call him, at home, right now—and threaten him." Lee was making a face of dread; Grace asked, "You don't think I should?"

"Calling's one thing. Maybe don't threaten."

"Threatening's the whole point, Lee. I want ulcer, bile, loss of sleep." She stubbed out her cigarette and snapped her fingers. "You know what, actually? Fuck it, fuck this, fuck him, let's get threatening." She scooted from the booth and stood before Lee with her hand out. "Change," she said, and Lee gave her some change, and she went away, returning five minutes later looking ashen, exhaling, shaking her head. "Outclassed me."

"He's a better threatener than you?"

"Much better."

"What happened?"

"I called him and he picked up and I said good evening and he said good evening and I performed my threats."

"Which were what?"

"Destruction of career, in a nutshell. Bit of a ramble. But my point was made, and I represented myself as sincere. He didn't make a peep until after I was done. When he spoke, his voice was calm, almost kind-sounding. 'Don't you understand, Grace, that it would be the easiest thing in the world to have you locked up for the rest of your life? That I could have you lobotomized with the flourish of my pen?'"

"Is that true?"

"It's true and he knows I know it's true because I've seen him do it."

"So what did you say?"

"I said, 'You make a good point.'"

"Then what?"

"Then I got off the goddamned phone."

"And now what?"

"Now forget it, he wins, I'm done. You want another drink?" Lee said he did, and he watched his sister cross the room and disappear into the crowd surrounding the bar. Moments passed, and Lee was lost in thought when a gaunt man with a goatee and hard-staring eyes approached the booth. He nodded at Lee as he sat. "That chick Grace asked me to talk to you." Leaning in, he said, "She tells me you got a little problem in your mailbox the other day."

"Okay," said Lee.

"She says that you're running."

Lee didn't say anything.

"Right," the gaunt man said. "Well, if you *were* running, or thinking of running, I want to talk to you about the alternative."

"And what's that?"

"You could stay."

"Stay and what?"

"Stay and fight."

"Fight who?"

"The people who sent you the letter."

"How?"

The gaunt man took a cigarette from Grace's pack and tucked it behind his ear. "We're creating a network of safe houses across the five boroughs for COs. There's a vetting process; and you'd be expected to put in hours on behalf of the effort. But if you're interested, I could bring your name to the committee."

"Put in hours how?"

"Day-to-day resistance work. Printing and distributing literature, organization of protests and happenings. Protests are the main thing. They're getting bigger every day but there are still a lot of people waffling. Your focus would be to get the stragglers to come down off the fence and join us in the streets. That's what it's all about now: the streets."

"The streets."

"Visibility in the streets."

"Right. And what happens if we're arrested?"

"We have access to lawyers working pro bono on behalf of the movement. I should say, and in the interest of full disclosure, that arrest is not unlikely. In a way, that's the aim."

"To be arrested."

"Yeah."

"What's the point of that?"

"To illustrate the consequences of independent thought in the United States of America. The whole world is watching."

"So what?"

"What?"

"What's the world going to do?"

"You want a simple answer to that?"

"Or a complicated one."

"Global opinion is relevant. Shame is a blunt but useful tool. Newspapers in every language on the planet are reporting on stateside war resistance and the public is increasingly on our side."

"But I mean, when I'm sitting in jail, what's the world going to do for me?"

"What will running do for you?"

"I won't have to deal with all the bullshit."

"Okay, so you get clear of that, and you stop running, and then what? What if you discover you're not the same person you started out as? Do you know what I mean?"

"I keep hearing this," Lee said. "But I have an alternative theory."

"And what's that?"

"I'll be exactly the same."

"You don't think running is going to do something to your spirit?"

"My spirit?"

"We're defined by our behaviors, by the choices we

make. To run is to degrade yourself. Here, think of it this way: you turn on the kitchen light and what happens? The cockroaches scatter."

"You're saying I'm a cockroach?"

"I'm saying you're *not* a cockroach. Why behave like one? The desire to avoid danger is hardwired into our brains from the days of the dinosaurs. But we don't live in caves anymore, man. We have free will, we have the strength of numbers. At some point we're all going to have to stand up and be counted."

"By who?"

"By our brothers and sisters." The gaunt man looked suddenly put-upon. "Look, are you cool?" he asked.

"What do you mean?"

"I mean, are you *cool*?"

"I don't think I am cool, no."

"Then why are we talking?"

"I really don't know."

A loud group burst into the bar and the gaunt man startled and turned to look, as did Lee. When Lee looked back, the gaunt young man was watching him with a wary expression. "You expecting someone?"

"No. Are you?"

"Why would I be expecting someone?"

"A man with your charisma must have a lot of friends."

"Is that a joke?"

"It's a joke."

"I'm not laughing."

"I could really give a fuck."

"You're out of line."

"Get the fuck out of my booth."

The gaunt man stood. "Nothing in this room is yours, man," he said, and walked off.

Grace approached the table with a beer in each hand, staring after the gaunt man as he walked away. "Where's Chucky going?"

"You know, he didn't say," said Lee.

"Were you rude to him?"

Lee made the little-bit gesture.

"Can't I take you anywhere?"

"Nowhere."

"Are you hungry?"

"I could be."

They finished their beers and walked to an Automat at Union Square. Lee had never seen an Automat before and was impressed by the tall wall of food options, each in its own temperature-appropriate glass-and-metal cube, the very visual of American convenience, vulgar bounty, but also a game to play. Grace got a slice of apple pie and a cup of coffee, Lee a bowl of chicken soup and a roll. They sat at a long table, thirty feet from one to the other end, but only three feet across, with a line of bolted stools running up both sides. Lee dipped his roll in his soup, but the roll was so stale it would not be softened. "My roll is impervious to liquid," he said, and Grace, looking at nothing, answered that that was fascinating and outrageous. A man sat down across from Lee wearing a shirt similar to one he had. "Don't let me forget to pick up my laundry on the way home," he said to Grace, and she replied that she absolutely would not forget—that she could never forget. Now Lee saw that the man was the wino from the laundromat, and that he was in fact wearing Lee's shirt. "Excuse me," Lee said, and the wino, chewing with stern concentration on a saltine, looked up.

"Remember me?"

"I don't believe I do, no. Have we met before?"

"We have, yeah. At the laundromat, about an hour and a half ago?"

The man was studying Lee's features. "I *was* at the laundromat," he admitted. But he shook his head. "I'm sorry, I just don't recall it." He held out his hand and asked, "How are you?"

Lee shook the man's hand. "I'm all right, thank you." He pointed. "That's my shirt you've got on."

The wino's chewing slowed. He swallowed, dabbed his face with his napkin. Looking down, he rested his palms on his shirtfront. "Oh my goodness," he said. "I think you may be right." His manner spoke of genuine bafflement, and Lee could see the man was living in some half-lit realm where only certain aspects of reality were available to him. Lee, drunk and high and tired to his bones, found the man's attitude perfectly charming. At the wino's elbow was the newspaper, refashioned into a neatly made package; Lee pointed at this and asked, "Is that the rest of it?" The wino, not knowing for certain, peeled back the edge of the paper and nodded. He pushed the package across the table to Lee and Lee opened it and made an inspection. Everything was tidily folded, socks matched and mated, but his chinos were missing, and he ducked his head under the table, dismayed to see the wino was wearing these as well. He'd not ripped the inseam but rather forced the bloated ankle through the leg so that the pant appeared inflated, and the material was damp with leg rot. "Oh, boy," said the wino, shaking his head at himself, or perhaps at man's fate, the immeasurable folly of the species. Lee was disappointed at the ruination of the chinos but soon recovered his good cheer, and he made a gift of the ensemble to the wino, and the wino was moved. Later he walked Lee and Grace to the door, shaking Lee's hand and advising the pair of them, "Have good times in the future."

Lee and Grace walked down Fifth Avenue and through the crowds in Washington Square Park. At Grace's encouragement Lee began a reverent recitation of the Pledge of Allegiance in his Donald Duck voice, a joke from their childhood. By the time they got back to the apartment, Grace was saying that she would come along with Lee to Canada. Lee didn't want this but he knew she wouldn't actually come, and wasn't concerned when she began packing up her suitcase. He slept on the sofa. In the morning his head hurt, and he drank coffee, and watched Grace unpack. She asked what he felt like doing that day, but all at once he had the sense of wanting to get the border crossing over with, and he told her he couldn't stay. She asked, "Do you want me to go to New Jersey with you?" "Why would I go to New Jersey?" "The car's going to New Jersey." "No, it's not." He kissed her bruised cheek and she hugged him and told him to call when he got somewhere worth discussing.

He took a white cross and drove the Jaguar eight hours to the border at Buffalo, where something unexpected happened, which was that he was denied entrance to Canada. He had not prepared any patter at all, and the fact of his not knowing where he was headed or to what purpose landed him in secondary inspection, a vast and hangar-like area filled with cars in states of undress. Lee was directed to a small office, where a border agent, fresh-faced and not unfriendly, asked if he was running from the draft, and Lee said he was not. The border agent asked him to stay put while he inspected the Jaguar, and Lee afterward watched through the glass as the agent unloaded his suitcase onto a long metal table set to the side of the car. He unpacked and inspected the suitcase, calm in his work, unhurried and thorough, and he took care to put things back as he found them. Once the suitcase was returned to the trunk, the agent moved to sit in the passenger seat and began looking through the glove box. When he discovered the draft notice he stepped from the Jaguar, whistled once, and held it above his head; his colleagues, scattered about the inspection area, cheered and jeered. They were all very young men, younger than Lee, even. A happy group; Lee's being caught in a lie gave them a sense of efficiency, and so they liked him. They sent him back to the United States with fond farewell wishes and Lee sat up very straight as he drove away from the border, impressed and sobered by the rejection. Ten miles outside of Buffalo he saw a cheap motel and pulled over for the night.

A BIRD OR AN ARROW

IN THE MORNING LEE DISCOVERED HE HAD ONLY TWO white crosses left. He took one and drove to the north and east, tracing the border along upper New York State and into Vermont, winding, two-lane country roads crowded by lush trees and foliage, green grasses, with wispy fog creeping across the pavement and blotting out the sun. He wasn't worried that he'd been turned away from the border, wasn't concerned by his not knowing what to do next. He was not desolate; he was calm, watchful of the era, fascinated. He had been driving for more than six hours when he pulled over at a pancake house, neon signage flashing FAMILY DINING and UNLIMITED

MAPLE SYRUP. The parking lot was empty; he sat in the Jaguar awhile thinking of this and that, recalling the faces he'd seen across the past week, and wondering how these people felt when they lay down in the dark to take their rest.

He entered the pancake house and took a seat at the counter. He put in an order for coffee and a slice of cherry pie, then sought out a phone booth. He called Cal but no one answered. He called Grace but no one answered. Someone had written *Lyndon Johnson Is a Shitmaster* on the wall beside the phone. Lee had no emotional response to the statement, but it conjured the hieroglyphics conversation he'd had with his mother, and so he called her, and she picked up and he said hello and she said, to him, "It's Leland." He explained that a piece of graffiti had brought her to mind. She asked him what it said and he told her.

"He is a shit*master*," she said. "And what is that, exactly?"

"I don't really know, Mom."

"But to be such a thing as this, it's no great achievement, I don't think."

"No, it's not meant as a compliment."

"Yes, well," Lee's mother said, "that this is the declaration that summoned me is unfortunate, but I'm glad you've called, because there's something I want to say to you. I've given your situation and behaviors some long and serious thought, and Wallace and I have had our bloody battle about it, and I have decided, or he has convinced me, that what you do is wise. Not to say that I'm doubled over with pride about it, but neither am I sickened with shame. My point is, I am at peace with your choices, and you may find solace in that, or not, per your heart's needs."

"Okay, Mom," said Lee. Actually, he was relieved at his mother's reversal; the truth was that he had been very much bothered by the thought of her disapproval.

She asked Lee, "Where are you?"

"Vermont."

"Why Vermont, and where?"

"It's just where I've wound up. I don't know what town I'm in but I'm calling from a pancake house."

"I see," she answered. "And you're planning on eating some pancakes, is that what you're telling me?"

"No, I'm having a coffee and pie."

"Isn't that nice?"

"Sure it is," said Lee.

"When will you cross the border?"

"I think soon."

"Today?"

"Yes."

"Shall I let you go?"

"Yes, but not yet. What's happening over there?"

"Oh, it's a day. I've got some weeding to do. Wallace is napping. We've a plan to cut one another's hair, but that might be pushed off until tomorrow. Do you know, I think Wallace is a little depressed since you've gone?"

"What's the matter?"

"Just that you brought a bit of pizzazz, which now is lacking. Wallace thought you a romantic figure, and that your suffering was attractive, and that someone ought to write a moody ballad about you. He'd have jumped right into the car if you'd asked him to come along."

"But not you?"

"Who would do the weeding?"

"Right."

"Will you call me when you've landed in Canada?"

"Yes."

"Here is what I'm hoping you'll be able to tell me: what city you're in, what you've eaten for dinner, and that you're safely installed in a rented room with a sturdy dead bolt, do you understand?"

"I understand."

"Even if you get in late, I want you to call and let me know you've settled in."

"All right."

"You're promising me?"

"I'm promising."

Lee said goodbye and returned to his seat. He ate the pie and drank the coffee and the waitress brought the bill and Lee paid but didn't leave. It had begun to rain, hard; the parking lot was sizzling and the diner was imbued with a to-the-side-of-time feeling that provoked Lee to linger.

The weather reminded Lee of Cal, and the way they always hid out in his apartment whenever it would rain. There was a pleasing sadness that came into the air when it rained at the beach, like an amusement park chained at the gate, dark-faced, closed for the season. Lee remembered it had been raining like this during the phase of days which came to be defined by Cal's abortion, and the time just after the abortion, when she stayed in Lee's apartment.

Six months into their relationship, and on the afternoon preceding the arrival of the rains, Cal came to see Lee and found him napping on the couch. She woke him up and he saw that something was the matter; there was something of the official visitor about Cal, and she had a distant look in her eye. She explained that she was pregnant, and was going to have an abortion in two days' time. Lee sat up and had only just started to make his protestation when Cal told him, "This is a monologue, Leland Clarke. There's not going to be a baby. And there's not going to be a discussion about there not being a baby. That's the full shape of it and I'm telling you to leave it alone." Lee must have looked particularly aggrieved; Cal's face turned kind, and she told him nothing would be different between them unless he wanted it to be. He nodded that he understood. "But do you want it to be," she asked.

She came back three days later, pale and very weak. She wouldn't speak about the procedure, and wouldn't go to the hospital or free clinic, but she didn't want to be alone, and clearly needed caring for; Lee took the week off work to look after her. For the first three days she was low, sleeping leadenly, eating little, and her waking moments were brief and without humor. There were bloody dressings in the bathroom trash can that frightened Lee; he was hopelessly out of his depth. But he fed her broth and would not let her smoke more than the occasional half cigarette and on the fourth day she began to brighten, her color returning, and she made a joke, which was to grip Lee's hand and say, "The world of man: a wasteland of scum." He understood the baby had likely not been his, or that it was not inarguably his; yet, and still, something changed for them after this, the relationship becoming realer. The tenderness Lee felt for Cal when he thought of her alone in some dark clinic or back room was a strong potion; and she had the sense that, along with the return of her strength, there was this other element the strength brought with it, a new style of happiness, so that afterward she no longer obscured herself from Lee, but faced him directly, to look at him, and to be looked at. All through this the rain was falling outside, days of it, heavy rain leaking into the apartment by the louvered windows, bending the parquet floor, and the sound of rushing streams down the street's gutters, pooling at the intersection at the bottom of the hill so that cars stalled out and the drivers cursed and wondered what to do. Lee and Cal were surrounded by the sound of moving water but there was a stillness in the apartment, and they spoke softly to one another, and they didn't know why.

Lee returned to the phone booth to call Cal. It rang ten times and he hung up but didn't leave the booth. The rain, and the reminiscence the rain had provoked, encouraged in Lee a sense of the maudlin, and he thought it as good a time as any to wallow in this, to punish himself by indulging in the thoughts he had been keeping at bay. These were framed around the general question of: What was Cal doing at that moment? What was happening just then, in her new life, with this new man? Propping his head against the face of the pay phone, Lee shut his eyes, that the pictures would be brighter in his mind. He decided Cal was at the boyfriend's apartment, and he tried to imagine the man, his dimensions, and the dimensions of his home. But other than a floating black mustache and carpeting the color of pureed baby food, Cal's new-life portrait remained opaque.

Cal herself came more easily to mind. Lee could clearly see her walking around in a sheet, in the hazy seaside morning light, grumbling under her breath. But this placed her in his apartment, with each detail at hand. Abandoning his exercise of self-punishment, then, and feeling a need to be near her, Lee began to watch a movie of Cal as she once had been: stepping from his kitchen to the living room, curling up on the couch, a can of beer in her hand. "A gentleman would fetch the lady an aspirin." These images, combined with Lee's tiredness, ushered him toward a sort of trance state, his mind a kite with its string cut. He thought of what Cal had told Robin about her new boyfriend: "You know him already, and you know he's not a motherfucker." The words, since he'd first heard them, had been worn away to meaninglessness; but now they stood up, and he suddenly had the idea that Cal was, at that same moment, alone in his apartment in Los Angeles. He dialed his own number and she picked up on the third ring. "Hello, he's not here."

"You love me basically," Lee said.

Cal paused. "I regret that," she said. "I've been regretting it."

"Okay but why can't you just say it?"

"It's hard to say. You say it."

"We're not talking about me; we're talking about you."

"All right, let's talk about me."

"How is it that you're answering my phone?"

"I've been sitting around here in a droop for the last five or six days. The phone rings and I pick it up thinking it might be you, though I don't know why it would be, because why would you call your own phone?"

"Yeah."

"Why did you?"

"I don't know. I guess I knew you'd be there, somehow."

"Okay, wow," said Cal.

"Who else has been calling?" asked Lee.

"Normally it's the furniture guy. The drive-away car guy's been calling a lot, lately."

"My old buddies."

"They're so disappointed in you. The car guy is desolate."

"I feel bad about the car guy."

"The furniture guy's less sympathetic."

"Yeah."

"Somebody called from the draft board."

"Checking on my health?"

"Confirming the date for your physical."

"And what did you tell them?"

"I told them you couldn't wait to get started."

"And what did they say?"

"That that's what they liked to hear."

Lee said, "So, you pick up my phone and Robin picks up your phone."

Cal said nothing. Lee thought of the face she was

likely making at this moment, a pinched grimace, sour, displeased. "You didn't know I knew, did you?"

"Did not know," she said.

"And how does it feel to know I do?"

"Well, not wonderful, obviously. But speaking on behalf of myself and for what it's worth I'd like to describe what happened with Robin as an unproud moment, which has not and will not be repeated. Beyond that, I suggest you zoom out for a minute and have a look at what I'm doing with my life. I've been haunting your apartment for most of this last week. Does that not mean something to you?"

"It does," Lee said. "I guess I just wish you hadn't fucked my friend fifteen minutes after I left town."

"It was a couple of days after. But I do apologize."

"Do you."

"I do."

"He seems very taken with you."

"Yeah, well, you know how it goes."

"I do know, yeah."

A silent moment. Cal asked, "So does that conclude the lecture or are we just pausing for refreshment?"

"I'm fine," Lee said.

"You're angry."

"It's going away."

"Is it?"

"Yeah."

"Okay, great." He heard her settling. "Why don't you tell me what's been going on?"

Lee explained that he'd been turned away in Buffalo and was tracing the border and would try to cross again, but that he didn't know where.

"Still aiming for Toronto?"

"I guess it's Montreal now."

"And how are you feeling?"

"More or less the same way I've felt since I left LA."

"Disappointed, bereft?"

"Yeah."

"Windswept?"

"Yeah."

"You been missing me?"

"Yeah."

"A lot?"

"Yeah."

Cal said, "Let no one say you don't know how to talk to a lady, Lee Clarke."

Lee said, "I *have* been missing you."

"Well okay. I have been, too." Cal thought a moment. "So are we ever going to see each other again, or what the fuck's happening?"

"We're going to see each other," said Lee.

"And how is that going to work?"

"I'm going to go wherever I'm going, get there, get a job, and send you a plane ticket."

"Is that right?"

"Yeah."

"And since when is that the plan?"

"Since just now."

"Think maybe you should sleep on it?"

"It'll be the same tomorrow."

"We'll see." Lee could sense Cal smiling as she spoke. "Is this plane ticket one way or round trip?"

"Whichever."

"Ambivalence, erotic."

"What I mean is, it's up to you."

"I should think it'd be up to both of us."

"I guess that's true."

"So which do you want?"

"You want me to tell you what I want?"

"I'll lie here comfortably on your you-smelling couch while you tell me what you want, yes."

Cal and Lee both were pleased. Each had been living with the belief that the other party had moved on, but now they understood they were wrong, and were savoring the toothsome relief of lost love returned. The operator came on the line and told Lee to add more change to continue the conversation but Lee had run out of coins. As the operator made her threats of disconnection, Lee talked over her, telling Cal he'd call her from Canada, and she asked if she should or should not pack her snowshoes and he told her to pack them, pack them, and the phone call was terminated, and Lee returned bouncily to the counter for another cup of coffee and the last white cross. The rain passed, the fog returned, no cars drove by—a long moment, without flaw. The waitress said, "You don't like to rush, do you," and Lee admitted he didn't. He asked if she wanted him to go and the waitress shrugged. It was a genuine shrug: she didn't care if Lee stayed or left.

Lee asked, "Where's the next border crossing?"

"Thirty miles east of here." She pointed to the east, then out the window and across the two-lane highway: a split rail fence, a long field climbing upward and to the edge of a forest. "But do you see the trees, there? That's Canada, more or less."

"What's past the trees?"

"There's a little town a couple miles in, but nothing much to look at until you get to Montreal."

Lee thought awhile, then called to the waitress for a pen and paper. "You going to write me a love poem?" she asked. She pulled a pen from her hair and ripped an unused page from her order pad. On the back of this, Lee wrote: *Contact the Four Winds Driveaway Company in Los Angeles, California*. He finished his coffee and left the diner, walking through the empty parking lot to the Jaguar. He pulled his suitcase from the trunk and left the keys and the folded note on the dashboard. Crossing the highway, he slid the suitcase through the split rail fence and climbed over. He started out across the field and toward the woods. The earth was wet and muddy and sucked at the heels of his shoes. The fog grew denser; he thought to wave at the unimpressible waitress but when he turned around the pancake house was no longer there. Following the upward grade of the field, he entered the woods, walking for fifteen minutes through paper birch and maple before coming out the other side and down a grassy hill to a paved road. He walked for thirty minutes in strange silence when an 18-wheeler drove slowly by. It had appeared from fog and disappeared back into it; a moment later Lee heard its air brakes come on as it pulled off the road. Soon he could make out the pink blush of neon through the gray scrim—the truck was parked out front of a bowling alley, which Lee entered. A kiosk beside the front door sold Canadian newspapers, candy, and cigarettes; a handwritten sign taped to the cash register read: AMERICAN MONEY AT PAR. On the wall was a framed portrait of the Queen of England.

A heavy man in denim and boots, whom Lee took to be the driver of the 18-wheeler, sat alone on a stool at the bar drinking a glass of red wine and smoking a cigar and assessing his mysteries. The bowling lanes were lit but empty; Lee studied them for a while. He decided bowling was a good and rational thing to do just then. To stand at the head of an avenue of long, polished wooden boards hefting a dense plastic sphere, to study on upsetting a triangulated formation of bottle-shaped pins, to topple them that they might be re-formed and toppled again. He rented a pair of bowling shoes from a shy teenaged boy with enflamed acne and horse teeth, then carried his suitcase to the center lane and sat to take his street shoes off, and to put the bowling shoes on. The bowling balls were smaller than the ones in the States; they fit in the palm and had no holes for his fingers. Also there were only five pins at the bottom of the lane, rather than the ten he was accustomed to. These little differences were both exotic and unnerving to Lee; they brought him to a place of understanding he was away from home now, that he had left his home for another place, and he did not feel any less himself, but didn't yet understand his position in the new landscape.

Later, Lee would find his way to Montreal, get himself a cheap hotel room, and sleep. The next day he would buy a newspaper and look for a job, a room to rent. He would read the marching lines of information, the impartial facts of the day. Once ingested and collated, the columns of ink would form a portrait: here was the world he was living in, here was the view from his small portion of allotted stage upon which he would perform the remainder of his life.

Lee selected a bowling ball and held it up to his chin

as he approached the lane. He breathed and stared at the pins; he drew a gently bending line in his mind. He wound up and released the ball, sent it scurrying down the buffed boards, then straightened and stepped back, waiting with no small interest to see how intention stood up against resistless power.